ANTHEM
FOR Jackson
Dawes

ANTHEM FOR Jackson Dawes

CELIA BRYCE

BLOOMSBURY
LONDON NEW DELHI NEW YORK SYDNEY

Bloomsbury Publishing, London, New Delhi, New York and Sydney

First published in Great Britain in January 2013 by Bloomsbury Publishing Plc
50 Bedford Square, London, WC1B 3DP

A CIP catalogue record for this book is available
from the British Library

ISBN 978 1 4088 2711 6

MIX
Paper from
responsible sources
FSC® C020471

Typeset by Hewer Text UK Ltd, Edinburgh
Printed in Great Britain by CPI Group (UK) Ltd, Croydon CR0 4YY

1 3 5 7 9 10 8 6 4 2

www.bloomsbury.com

For
Deanna Hall
1971–1979
and
Vaila Mae Harvey
1991–2008

Jackson Dawes
 He's as tall as doors,
   standing
    in his
     battered old hat,
   singing his
   battered old
    songs,
slapping his fingers down the length of the stand
like an upright bass.
 Badum, dum, dum, dum;
   badum, dum, dum, dum.
   His hips swing gently,
   his head nods,
   his smile is wide, big
    as
    the sun,
    as if this is just
     any other day, as if the world
      can't get any better,
     as if the future
    is brighter
    than
     stars.

    Megan Bright, Megan Silver,
  he sings in that way of his.
Megan Bright, Megan Silver...

One

'Now you know what I think of hospitals, so you can ring me any hour of the day or night.'

Grandad's voice seemed a long way off, making him sound even older than he was, making him sound as if he was on another planet instead of at the other end of a telephone.

It was Megan's first day in. 'Yes, I know,' she said, trying to sound brave, wanting everything to be better without having to be in hospital. She followed Mum through the double doors on to the ward, and stopped dead.

A baby ward?

That couldn't possibly be right.

But it was.

There were babies and signs of babies everywhere.

3

Toys being banged. Something rattling. Another thing chiming. Whirring. Squeaking. Somewhere off to the right there was a baby crying.

Just ahead a small child driving a plastic car headed off to the left. The horn beeped. An adult followed in deep conversation with a nurse.

Grandad was still talking, telling her not to worry, but Megan couldn't answer.

Where were the other patients? People like her? People her age?

She wasn't a baby or a toddler. She was almost fourteen!

Why had they put her here? How could they?

Text Gemma. As soon as possible. She'd know the answers. That's what best friends were for, wasn't it? To calm you down, talk you through things. Though with Gemma it was more a case of hugging you through things!

Dad liked Gemma. She didn't waste words. Not like some of Megan's friends. The Twins, for example, who would always use a hundred words when one was enough.

With Gemma it would be a ☺ or a ☹ and that would sum it all up.

Yes.

Text Gemma. Even she would have something to say about being put on a baby ward.

Grandad was still trying to be cheerful. 'They won't let me loose on a bus, so I can't come down . . . But if there's anything bothering you, lass, just tell them you have to call me. Tell them I'm the oldest man in the village, which means I know more than they do.'

Megan laughed because that's what he'd have wanted, but Grandad wasn't finished.

'In fact, if they need a hand with anything... washers for taps, spanners, wrenches, anything to do with plumbing...' he said.

'They probably have people to do things like that,' Megan interrupted, determined to keep the shake out of her voice. It wasn't easy. She could hear babies crying. She could hear the whine of toddlers. It occurred to her that she probably wasn't supposed to be using her mobile. It might interfere with things. Like on aeroplanes. If anyone noticed, they might take it off her. She clamped it closer to her ear. No way. Not before she reached Gemma. Oh, hurry up, Grandad. Ring off. Shut up.

But no. He was still trying to make it all turn out right, trying to fix things the way he always had when he ran his hardware shop.

He could fix just about anything, could Grandad.

'Well then, *you* know where I am.' He sounded even further away. 'But it'll be fine, you'll see, sure as eggs is eggs. Bye for now, Pet Lamb.'

Eggs is eggs. Yeah. Well.

It was horrible. The whole thing. Having cancer was bad enough, since it wouldn't go away on its own, but really? A baby ward?

And the hospital was miles away from home. It meant that Mum had a lot of driving to do in the city. She hated city traffic and you couldn't ever find a place in the hospital car park.

It was just going to be too difficult, the whole thing.

'Well,' Mum said, 'this isn't bad, is it?'

Megan twisted her face. 'It's not good.'

'Of course . . . obviously it's *not* good, having to be here, but when you're poorly . . .'

'Yes, I know, but . . .' Megan stopped. But what? Exactly? What did it matter if the place was full of babies, full of toddlers? She had cancer and had to have it sorted out.

Yet it did matter.

Somehow it *mattered*.

'Never mind,' Mum said, keeping bright, like the colours around them both, on the walls, on the ceiling, wherever you looked. Nothing stayed too terrible for long according to Mum. 'There'll be lots to tell Dad when he rings. He'll want to know what's what.' Then her voice changed, the cheeriness disappearing, as if it was too hard to keep it going for ever. Like balloons at a party. They always went down, eventually. 'I wish . . .'

Megan knew what was coming. Her stomach tightened as if she'd just swallowed a bowl of cement. She didn't want to hear it. 'Dad doesn't need to be here. I've got you.' Trying to be cheerful. 'And I've got Grandad. I'll be all right.'

Mum sighed. 'Yes, you've got me and Grandad.' She managed a small laugh. 'And he's threatened to phone every day. Twice a day if he has to. I feel sorry for the nurses. He'll be checking up on them, just watch.' She shook her head. 'As if he knows the first thing about hospitals. About this sort of place, anyway.'

A curly-haired toddler came racing towards them on his bottom. He was being chased by his curly-haired brother who picked him up with a struggle. Then his curly-haired mother appeared, her cheeks pink, a deep frown on her face.

'Careful with him, Dylan, *please!*'

The toddler giggled as if this was the funniest thing ever. His mother smiled a tight kind of smile.

'Welcome to the madhouse,' she said, scooping up her son, who whooped in delight. She gave Megan a sympathetic look. 'Don't worry, love, we won't be here for too much longer! Peace does happen sometimes.'

'Whoa!' Something from behind hurtled into her, big hands gripping her shoulders. 'Sorry!' The *something* was a boy, tall as anything, in a big T-shirt and baggy jeans. 'I'm trying to see how fast you can push one of these. Important scientific research. See ya!'

Sidestepping Megan and her mother, he steamed on ahead with his drip stand. There were four bags of fluid hanging from it and tubes like spaghetti tumbling into two blue boxes clamped on to the stand.

7

'Oh . . . well . . .' Mum looked vague. 'Research.'

'I don't think so,' Megan said, 'and I don't need any more help to make me dizzy. How stupid is he?' She took Mum's arm because now she was feeling quite wobbly. 'Oh no. He's back.'

Sure enough, the boy was heading their way once more.

'Hey, *you're* not a baby!' The drip stand squeaked as he pushed it along. He gave her a huge grin. 'You're normal!'

What did he expect, a Martian?

'Say hello, love. Where's your manners?' Mum whispered, nudging her.

'He's just collided into me,' Megan muttered. 'Where're his?'

The boy was checking her out as if he'd never seen a girl before. Or had seen too many, and knew just where to look. Scowling, Megan folded her arms, wishing Mum had made her put on a thicker top.

'We're new here,' Mum said, bright as light bulbs. 'Don't know where we're going really, just told to . . . you know . . . turn up!' She threw her arm around Megan's shoulder and squeezed, as if this was the first day at Butlin's.

Shrugging her off, Megan looked at the boy, tall as doors, taller even, with a hat pulled down low like a gangster in a film. His eyes were dancing. He was laughing at her. Probably not even on this ward and just here to gloat. Well, let him.

8

The boy was just about to say something when two little girls came down the corridor, arms linked, heads close, talking giggly secrets. They stopped and gazed, sparkle-eyed, first at the boy, then at Megan.

'Jackson,' said one, her voice high-pitched, her face alive with excitement, 'got a new girlfriend?'

He shook his head, tutted. 'Becky, Becky, Becky! Give us a high five,' he said. They high-fived. 'Who's your friend?'

'Laura.'

'Well, here's one for you too, Laura.' He high-fived the other girl. More giggles rang along the corridor.

Was he playing with *nine-year-olds*? Sixteen, seventeen, maybe, and hanging out with *nine*-year-olds? Megan picked at a speck of fluff on her sleeve, but it wouldn't come off. Mum was smiling so much her cheeks were two red balls.

They should be unpacking. The nurses might be waiting or a doctor. Someone should be told she'd arrived. Yet there they were still in the corridor, with all its cartoons and *him* standing in the middle of it, the star of the show.

Megan pressed into the wall, like a shadow.

More giggles behind hands clamped to mouths. The boy looked down at the girls like a school prefect, the girls looked back up expectantly, as if this had all happened before, as if they knew what was coming next, as if it was all just a big game.

9

'Will you tell us a spooky story, Jackson? Laura wants to hear one. Will you?'

Megan rolled her eyes.

'Not right now. Go on, Becky. Aren't you meant to be visiting your brother? Isn't that why you're here . . . ?'

The girls looked at each other as if they'd just remembered. 'Whoops! OK. See you later!' Overcome with laughter, they bumped along the walls towards the main ward. Jackson shook his head then turned back to Megan, checking her out once more. She looked the other way.

'Quite a fan club you've got there!' Mum said, giggling like a girl, as if she wanted to be part of it too.

The boy laughed. 'Something like that.'

Megan stuffed her hands into her pockets and examined a picture on the wall. It was a fat elephant. Flying. It had three pink toenails on each foot.

There was a tap on her shoulder. It was the boy. 'So, what's *your* name?' he asked.

Megan turned to face him, but didn't answer.

'Oooh, she's lost her tongue all of a sudden. This is Megan and I'm her mother. High five, Jackson!'

'Mum! Don't we have to *go* . . . ? I'll need to sign in or something.'

'Yes . . .' Mum was still smiling, still gazing at Jackson.

'They do need to know I'm here, don't they?' What was it about this boy that had everyone going all gooey?

A movement in the corridor made them turn.

'Uh-oh! Sister Brewster . . .'

Coming towards them was a tall woman, with hair like wire. It was short and grey and made her look like a head mistress. Under her arm was a bundle of folders. She stopped and turned startlingly blue eyes to Jackson, who was suddenly silenced. Megan shifted her gaze back to the elephant's pink toenails, trying to stifle a laugh. Not such a big star now.

'Jackson . . . at least let the girl settle in. She's not had a chance to catch her breath!'

Megan sensed that Sister Brewster wouldn't be messed with. Jackson obviously knew it too. With a sheepish shrug, he took off his hat and gave a slight bow. He was completely bald. Mum's mouth fell open.

'Polished it this morning, just for you coming in,' he said, grinning and putting his hat back on.

'Yes. Thank you, Jackson. Show's over.' Sister Brewster moved to one side to let him past. 'You have a visitor.'

Jackson gave them all a wide grin. 'See you later,' he said, striding down the corridor, hips swinging, long legs almost bouncing him away and his drip stand trundling along beside him.

Sister Brewster shook her head and sighed. 'Completely starved of company since he got here.'

As he headed away, a door swung open and out stepped a small lady wearing a black hat with a feather, a thick yellow coat and a face like thunder. She stood with her hands on her hips, round as a dumpling.

'Jackson? You come right here, boy, disturbing the peace like some hooligan.' Her voice was loud and gravelly, not to be ignored.

Jackson stopped and turned back to face Megan. 'Meet my mother . . .' he said. 'I don't know how she does that. Showing up at just the wrong time. How does she do that?'

Megan shrugged a haven't-a-clue kind of shrug. *Serves him right. Big-head.*

'Can't let a poor girl even find her room without you getting in the way. Come here this second, boy.'

'All right, all right!'

Jackson's mother stood by the door, waiting until he was back in the room. She marched in after him.

'*That boy,*' Mum said, 'is just beautiful. He's like an ebony statue. And that smile . . . it just never stops. Isn't he lovely . . . ?'

'That boy,' Sister Brewster said, 'could use a distraction, and I think he's found one.' She nodded meaningfully at Megan.

No way. No. Way.

Megan hadn't liked the consultant's room. It was down in Outpatients and it was where they told her she had cancer. It wasn't like a real doctor's room. Her *own* doctor had pictures of his children on the wall. Three boys, all the same age. A nightmare in triplicate, he called them.

He had funny little toys on his desk to keep little patients amused. She remembered going there when she was small; she remembered the tiny monkey which crawled up his stethoscope, or it would have done if it was real. She remembered thinking that he was the nicest doctor in the world. On the wall above his examination couch he had an enormous photograph of some mountains, all covered in snow, like a ski resort. He looked as if he was always just about to go on holiday, her own doctor. Cheerful, full of fun.

The consultant was about as much fun as a carton of warm milk. He had half-moon glasses and when he smiled, which wasn't very often, he looked like a frog. His room had bare walls and too many doors. He had a nurse whose mouth looked too small for her face. She came in one of the doors with a pile of folders, which she put on his desk, then she disappeared through another door. Megan had no idea where they all led to. *She'd* come in from the Red Area waiting room, through the *sick children's* entrance. Everyone who came through that door was supposed to be poorly, whether they felt it or not.

Maybe it was to do with all of this that Megan laughed until she almost wet herself, when he said she had a tumour and the tumour was cancer. It was a mistake, obviously. She didn't feel ill for a start.

She looked at Mum and Dad to see if they realised that it was all a mistake too, but they just sat quietly, side by side, like those things Grandad had to stop his books falling over. Bookends, he called them.

She hadn't been ill, just dizzy at times. A bit wobbly. How could it be cancer? It was stupid. She would just go home and forget about it. Easy-peasy.

Anyway, what did *he* know?

The consultant twiddled with his pen until she'd finished laughing, but just as he was about to say something, Megan fired one question after another at him, as if she'd been saving them up for weeks and had to get them all out. She left no space for answers. Would she still be able to play football? And go to the ice rink? Would she still be able to go to the cinema with her friends? Would she still be able to go shopping? What about school? Would the tumour go away by itself? Why had it happened?

At last the questions dried up. All of that activity made her tired. Megan slumped back in the chair and could think of nothing else to say or do.

She noticed how the consultant was examining the blotter on his desk.

She noticed how still Mum and Dad were, like statues, how they were holding hands.

'I realise it's a shock to be told this,' the consultant said at last, 'and I'm very sorry that the tests couldn't have given better news.' He flipped open a folder, which must have been Megan's. There seemed to be a lot of pages. A lot of tests. 'But now that we know, and we're sure about it, we can think about how to treat you.'

Treat me? With chocolate? Ice cream? New clothes? Don't think so, somehow.

'I think what we'll do is try some chemotherapy and that should make it easier to remove.'

'How do you do that?' Megan asked. Her mind had gone completely blank. 'How do you remove a tumour?'

The consultant seemed taken aback. 'We do an operation,' he said.

'You mean, cut my head open?'

'Yes, Megan. That's exactly what I mean.'

But why, when she didn't feel ill? Why didn't Frog-Man get his head cut open? Check there was a brain in there, because he'd got it all wrong. He must be thinking about some other patient. Probably that stupid nurse with the little mouth had given him the wrong file. There was probably another Megan Bright. That's what had happened.

Easy-peasy. Lemon-squeezy. And yet, she began to shiver. It wasn't cold in the room, but she was trembling all over. Someone took her hand. It was Dad. She had to check, because everything was feeling very strange now. She felt like a foreigner, someone who didn't understand the language, someone who'd do anything to hear something familiar.

The consultant gave his frog smile. '. . . I think we

can feel very positive about your treatment, Megan. I want you to know that.'

Like waving a magic wand. Yeah. Right.

'So, an operation?' That was Mum, twisting her handkerchief between her fingers. It was a small lace-edged thing with a green shamrock sewn into the corner. She sounded as though she'd just fallen into the room from another place and wasn't sure about anything much.

'When?' Megan asked.

'I can't say at this stage,' the consultant replied. 'But you will have to come in as soon as we can find you a bed.' He closed Megan's folder. Was it a sign for them all to go?

No one moved. Everyone just waited for what would happen next.

At last Dad gave a little cough. He squeezed Megan's hand. 'How does that sound?' he said.

It sounded rubbish.

The bright pink suitcase sat like one of those flowers that grow in the desert after the rain. Mum was putting things away, arranging them the way she arranged everything. Clothes were folded into neat parcels and placed, with meticulous care, into the locker, as if it mattered a great deal where they went.

Standing by the bed, Megan wished Mum would stop. *Don't do that, not yet*, she wanted to say. *I need to do it – my way, when I want to. They're my things.*

The words were there, but they stuck in her throat, swelling up inside her.

At last, everything was in place, the locker packed with pieces of Megan's life, all ordered and hidden behind the doors. Mum's cheeks were flushed. She was gazing around the room as if taking it all in, or maybe just wondering what to do or say next, hating to be idle.

'If only your dad was home,' she said, out of the blue. 'He wanted to come, be here with you.'

It was enough to un-stick everything. Megan exploded. 'No!' 'He has a job to do and it's too far away. He'll phone, email. You can print them off. I don't *want* him to come.' Megan stopped, realising that she was shouting, but gave the room a disgusted look. 'It's not as if there's a computer *here*.'

Deep breath in, deep breath out. Keep calm, don't lose it now.

Yet with the breathing in and the breathing out, all her strength seemed to go; it just seeped out of her. Not even her eyes would stay open; they were too full, too heavy. She *did* want Dad, she wanted him so much it hurt, but he mustn't come. She had made him promise. Made him cross his heart. He mustn't do anything different. He worked away, that was normal; he came home on leave, when it was his turn, and that was normal.

He had to keep it all the same.

That way, *that way*, she would get better. 'I'm fine,' she said, her voice quiet, controlled. 'He doesn't need to be here. And neither do you.'

An Irish nurse called Siobhan came in to see if they were all right. They weren't, not really, but at last, after a cup of tea and a little more fussing, Mum said she might think about going home for a few hours.

'You can stay,' Siobhan said. 'There's a pull-down here.' She indicated the extra bed folded like a broken wing against the wall next to Megan's. 'Parents do.'

If I was little, yes, if I was a baby. 'Tomorrow, Mum. Come back tomorrow. I'll be fine. Really, I will.'

She watched an exchange of glances between Mum and the nurse, who suggested that Mum could stay while she had some blood taken.

'They'll be starting your treatment.' Mum exchanged another glance with the nurse. 'I should stay.' Megan gave them a look, a shake of the head. 'All right,' Mum said, 'I'll leave it till tomorrow. But first thing, I'm coming back. And you have to ring if you want me in sooner. Any time, mind you.'

At last Mum was on her way out, still fussing, still not wanting to leave. 'Why not talk to that boy? He'll know all there is to know about the ward and everything.' Megan refused to acknowledge her. 'You could be friends, love.'

'I've got friends. I'm fine.'

18

As soon as Mum went home, Megan yanked out every single one of her belongings, surrounding herself with them. She sat like a hamster in the middle of its nest. They were private things, *her* things, letters from Dad, make-up, underwear. Everything. She wanted them around her for a little longer, wanted to feel them still, these small fragments of home. They were part of her, they told her who she was.

Megan looked at the sink, the shelf above it, the bin below, the bed with all of its levers and pedals, the TV on a stem growing from the wall behind, the whiteboard with a name written in big blue letters. Her name. Somehow that was a surprise.

Two

'So, Megan Bright,' Jackson read out her name from the doorway, 'homesick yet?'

'No.'

Shoving her things into a rough pile, Megan threw her dressing gown over the lot to hide them. It was a green dressing gown, making her bed look as if it had grown a hill. Something about that was satisfying – it made her feel slightly better. This was her own hill and only she was allowed to climb it or dig into it, nobody else.

'Can I come in? Just got a refill.' Jackson indicated the fattest bag of fluid hanging from the drip stand.

Megan slid her eyes from his grinning face and looked at the green hill on her bed, smoothed out the folds, patted it down.

'Well, can I?' Jackson leaned up against the door frame.

'I thought you'd be too old for a baby ward,' Megan said, 'with your important scientific research and everything.'

Jackson sighed. 'Sorry. Didn't mean to run you over, but it gets so boring, it does your head in. Rooster reckons –'

'*Who* reckons?'

'Sister Brewster. Says as long as I don't bug you, then it's OK for me to come and say hello, us being the only *teenagers* in the whole wide world.' He spread his arms, making a dramatic sweep.

Megan fiddled with the belt of her dressing gown.

'Honest. This ward is the world. And we're the oldest in it. Only they don't treat you like it. You need *parental permission* to get out. Just to the shop! You wouldn't believe it.' Jackson plonked himself down in the chair next to her bed. He settled down in it, long-legged, almost too big for the place, like a trapped bird in a cage too small. His gaze settled on the green hill of belongings, then on Megan. 'And they make you do school. It's hopeless.' He stopped. 'I've just talked too much, haven't I?'

Megan didn't answer, just slid her hands to the pile, wanting to hug it to her, protect it, never let it go. Her eyes began to sting.

'What you got under there, anyway?' Jackson leaned forward.

'Don't!' Megan pulled her belongings towards her. The dressing gown slid off slightly, revealing the edges of stuff, corners, bits of underwear. She felt naked, him being there looking at her things like that, like some perv. 'Leave them alone. They're mine.' She covered them up once more, smoothing out the creases.

Jackson held up his hands, all long fingers. 'All right! I'm not touching anything, see?' He shook his head, smile all gone. 'Rooster says . . .'

'She says nothing about just turning up like you own the place, or running people over in corridors, or being nosy about private things.'

Jackson shrugged. 'She was on about being friends.'

'Got some. Thank you.' There was a long silence which she wasn't going to break.

'You'll be disappointed,' Jackson said at last. 'Friends mess you about.'

'Mine won't,' Megan said. 'They're going to bring stuff.'

Jackson shook his head. 'They'll think they're going to *catch* something. They won't say it, but they'll look at you like there's bits dropping off and it's going to happen to them if they get too close. You'll see.'

Typical boy. *His* friends might be like that, but *hers* weren't. 'You don't know everything.'

Jackson lounged in the chair as if he did indeed

know everything, especially her friends. He crossed his legs, uncrossed them. Two slashes of skin grinned through the frayed rips in his jeans.

Megan picked up the corner of her dressing gown, let it drop.

Her friends *would* come.

'Too much homework,' Jackson went on. 'Too much to do. They're grounded. Live too far away. Band practice. I know all the excuses.'

Megan looked at him. '*Band practice?*'

Jackson knitted his fingers, studying them for a few seconds. 'We used to have a band going, me and my mates. They've got to keep rehearsing, so they can't come. That's their story, anyway.'

'Rehearsing without you?'

'Well, *I'm* here, *they're* there,' he said, 'and *that's* that.' He began to chew at his nails, at the skin around them.

More silence.

Megan glanced at her bed, wishing that she hadn't hauled everything out of her locker. It would take ages to put it all back.

'I'm bugging you, aren't I?' Jackson pushed up his hat with a finger. Megan shrugged an answer. 'Is that a yes or a no?' He was looking at her with his huge brown eyes, jutting out his bottom lip, like a baby about to cry.

Becky and Laura might think that was funny. His *fan club*. Nine-year-olds.

'My grandad's ringing. After his tea. He's ninety-five,' Megan said. Jackson gave her a blank stare. 'It's a big thing for him.' She stiffened her voice. 'And he will ring.'

'OK, I get the message. I'm out of here.' Jackson slid from the chair and was by the door in one smooth movement. He peered out, then turned to face her. 'Ever slept with a drip?' Megan blinked. Jackson nodded at the bags of fluid attached to him.

She shook her head. 'Don't worry. You get used to it.'

Something in his voice made her look at him. His eyes were hidden by the brim of his hat, most of his face too. She could see the curve of his lips, the angle of his jaw, his long neck, his fingers loosely holding the door. He tilted his head back against the door frame. She could see his eyes, the gleam in them.

'You'll get used to most things,' he said. 'Even me.'

Left alone, Megan gazed around the room, at its walls, its gleaming freshness, as if it had all been cleaned and polished ready for somebody new. She felt small, insignificant, not quite as clean and shining as everything around her.

'I'm here,' she whispered. 'Have you noticed me yet?'

Nothing moved, nothing stirred, not even the curtains at the open window.

Megan looked at the green hill on her bed and laid her head on top of it, feeling the outline of her things, her whole life in fragments, under the dressing gown.

* * *

'We've just got to get this going,' Siobhan said as she put up the chemo in its see-through bag, set the rate with the press of a button and checked the drops as they began to fall. There were lots of beeps and little lights. At last they settled into silence. 'That's it,' she said finally. 'All we have to do is wait for it to work.'

It was like watching one of those cookery programmes, with the TV chef talking through all the moves, from whisking eggs to adding salt and pepper.

And here's one I prepared earlier.

And now it was all done.

Siobhan washed her hands at the sink. She pulled a paper towel from the dispenser, dried her hands on it, then dropped it in the waste bin. 'After a few days, you'll go home and come back for the next lot . . . In three weeks, probably.'

Home after a few days. Back in after three weeks. What about everything else?

'You know school and stuff?' Megan said. 'Will I just go back when I get out?'

Siobhan wrote something on a chart. 'If you want to. If you feel OK. Some people do, some don't. It depends.'

Megan sighed.

'I know that's the vaguest answer in the world. But, you see, you're all so different and on different

treatments and for different lengths of time.'
Siobhan shook her head as if it were a huge problem. 'Now, if you pesky patients would just help by
having the same tumours, in the same places, it
would be a great advantage to the medical world.
We could all go home at teatime!' Siobhan swirled
her pen in the air as if it could cast a spell. 'Wouldn't
that be just magic!'

Megan smiled. She couldn't help it. 'But if I do go
back, what about the tube thingy, the line?'

'Listen, you and that line are going to become so
well acquainted you won't want to part with it. You'll
be the best of friends and have a bundle of laughs.'
Siobhan patted her arm and was serious again. 'We
leave it in, Megan, so's we're not sticking you with
needles all the time.'

'But I'm not supposed to get it wet?'

'If you mean swimming, then, no. But you can still
have a shower.'

'I can't see me playing football, doing PE . . .'

'As long as it's taped up, why not?' Siobhan said.
'Obviously, you don't want to yank the thing out.
But it's not for ever, you know. Really, it isn't.'

Megan gazed up at her drip and the tube, the drip
stand. 'Yeah, I know.'

Siobhan looked about to say something else when
she frowned. Someone was outside. 'Hello there,' she
said, leaning out of the door. 'Are you all right?
Where's your mammy?' Whispers. More movement.

'No, not at the moment, Kipper. Megan's busy right now . . .'

Kipper? What kind of name was that?

'. . . but maybe you can come back later? Off now, and I'll see you, soon as I've finished here. No, I'm sure Megan won't mind if you come and say hello some time.'

Siobhan smiled as she came back in. 'A little doll, that one. Loves Jackson to bits. Maybe she's wanting to size up the opposition.' She winked at Megan. 'You being it . . .'

Megan tutted. 'She's welcome to him. How old is she?'

'Nearly seven, bless her. She almost lives here.' Siobhan was tidying up, her movements quick and unfussy, as if she knew her job inside out. Within just a few seconds the place was just as it had been, except for the drip, of course, and the machine attached to it, with all of its numbers and the click of it and the blue casing.

Megan looked back up at it and watched as the clear drops formed with each click, watched as they grew and fell in a steady rhythm and was thankful that it wasn't for ever, that she didn't have to almost live on the ward. 'What do you tell the little ones to make them feel it's all just a bundle of laughs? What do you say to – Kipper?'

Siobhan smiled. 'Ah now, the little ones. They get the special treatment. They get the talk about the bad-guy cells and the good-guy cells and magic wands and wizards and it's all an adventure and they're the star of the show. Like a cartoon. But you, you just get it straight.'

Megan twiddled her name bracelet, pushing it around her wrist. She had a number all to herself, which made her unique. Yet not unique at all. 'Have we all got the same, then, on this ward? Have we all got cancer?'

'Yes,' Siobhan answered. 'Every single one of you.'

'How many's that?'

'Eighteen, when we're full. We have a baby in. Six months. Poor wee feller. He just lights up, though, when his sister comes in. That's Becky. I think you might have met her . . .' Siobhan was moving towards the door.

'And me and Jackson. We're the oldest?'

'You are. You're the big guys.'

'Fighting the bad guys.'

'That just about sums it up. But you're lucky, Megan. You can go home, you can go back to school even, between bouts.'

School. The very thought of it. It wasn't as if she was having her appendix out the way Frieda did and showed everyone her wound, or when Darren Longstaff broke his leg and came in with his plaster and crutches. It didn't feel the same somehow. It didn't feel like anything to boast about, having cancer.

'Mum says I don't have to. I can do work at home.'

'Or some do half-days, you know. It all depends. But there's no pressure, no need to worry about it now. You just concentrate on getting better. OK?' Siobhan gave a little wave. 'See you later. Just press the bell if you want anything.'

Out she went.

Megan slumped back on her pillows. Half-days. How were you supposed to keep your place on a football team with half-days?

'Now, I've got a whole village to keep informed of what they're doing to my girl in hospital, so give me lots of details, lass. Mrs Lemon's here listening, so I won't get it wrong when anyone asks.'

Grandad's voice sounded as it always did, old and tinny, hard to understand if you didn't know it or weren't used to listening to it. Megan could picture him, with both hands wrapped around the receiver, clinging on, as if it would fly away. She could see Mrs Lemon, his carer, making sure it didn't.

'I'm too tall for the bed,' she told him.

'You're a tall lass. That's only to be expected.'

'No, it's because the bed's too small. They're baby beds, almost.' He'd never understand, unless he was here to see it. How could he know what it was like?

'*Baby beds*,' Grandad told Mrs Lemon.

'But at least I've got a room to myself.'

She went on to describe the ward, Sister Brewster,

the doctors, Siobhan, then Jackson, starting with the fact that he was a right pain.

'And he tells ghost stories to *nine*-year-olds! But it just shows you what kind of ward we're on.' Even now the thought outraged her.

'So how old is he?'

'Dunno, but he mustn't be sixteen yet, or he'd be on the adult ward.'

'Is he friendly?' Grandad sounded concerned, as if she didn't have friends of her own. Why did everyone think she *needed* Jackson?

'Too friendly, if you ask me. He's got no hair.'

There was a little silence before Grandad answered. 'Well, now.'

Megan could hear Mrs Lemon in the background, maybe wanting to know what was wrong.

'*Jackson's got no hair*,' she heard Grandad say.

There was another silence. Then she heard something which might have been Mrs Lemon asking who Jackson was.

'Well, now,' Grandad said again. 'Does he suit it?'

'Mum thinks he's gorgeous.' As if that decided anything.

'Oh, well. That's good.'

Another silence.

Grandad must have been expecting her to say something else, or he'd run out of questions to ask, or answers to give – the man who had something to say about anything and everything usually. The

31

silence grew into a gap. Even Mrs Lemon had run out of noises to make.

'They've got elephants on the curtains,' Megan said at last. 'Elephants!'

'*She's got elephants.*' Grandad sounded relieved. There was an '*Oooh, fancy!*' from Mrs Lemon.

It was babyish, all of this kids' stuff, Disney World wherever she looked, and nurses wearing apron things with cartoons on them.

'And it's got stupid pictures all over the walls.'

'Well, what you have to do,' Grandad advised, 'is to ignore all of that stuff and nonsense and get better. What have you got to do?'

'Ignore all that stuff and nonsense and get better.'

'There's my girl. Tell yourself that, whenever you get sick of elephants. I would get sick of elephants,' he said, 'they make footprints in the butter.' Megan laughed, but just as suddenly she was crying.

'Now, now, I know my jokes are bad . . .'

'Worse than Dad's,' she managed.

'*Worse than her dad's.*'

Another little gap. Maybe it was dawning on Grandad that talking to him was OK, but talking to Dad would have been good too. More than good.

'Have you spoken to him yet? Has he managed to get through to you?' Megan couldn't speak. Grandad rushed on, suddenly having plenty to say. 'Can't be easy being out there in some Russian oilfield. Suppose there's not much in the way of telephones.

32

Too many people wanting to use them. Wouldn't rightly know, but I'd say that's the size of it.'

Even if she could have spoken, Megan couldn't explain even to herself why she'd made Dad promise not to ring while she was in hospital, except that he was always saying how difficult it was, being so far away. So she had told him to wait until she was home. It would be something to look forward to, she'd said when he tried to change her mind.

'It's the time difference, it's hard to get it right sometimes,' Megan said, wishing she'd never made Dad promise anything at all, she *so* wanted to hear his voice, so wanted to see him.

'I wonder,' Grandad said, 'I wonder what kind of birds he'll get out there? Should have sorted a book out for him before he went. Could have kept a list.' Grandad and his lists. 'That's what you can ask him when he phones. Tell him your grandad wants to know what he's seen. He'll need something interesting to do, fill in his time. *I'm saying he should watch birds.*'

There was a muttering in the background. Megan managed a giggle. Watching paint dry is how Dad described birdwatching. Maybe it was the same with Mrs Lemon.

'I'll tell him,' she promised.

There was a loud noise suddenly, a long drawn out wail, as if something horrible was happening to a baby in another room, then a phone rang and rang.

Just outside her door there was the scramble of feet, some loud voices, a stab of laughter, then silence once more.

'Wish I didn't have to be on a children's ward. Wish they'd let me be on an adult ward.'

'No, you don't,' came the reply. 'Full of old codgers. You wouldn't want that. Do nothing but complain, the lot of them. Nurse this, Nurse that. I should know. I was one of them.' He laughed then. 'Give them a right runaround, I did, even with my wrists in plaster.'

There was another gap full of silence, where maybe she was supposed to laugh, and allow him to tell her again about breaking his wrists doing the hokey-cokey.

More muttering in the background.

'*Yes, yes! I will* . . . Mrs Lemon wants to know if they've done anything to you yet?'

Megan didn't know where to start. There was so much, she couldn't remember what order it had all happened in, everything confusing, some of it just a bit frightening. 'I've got a drip,' she said, gazing up at the bag, the metal stand with its wheels, all part of her now, of this world she had to be in.

'That'll be for the pop, I suppose,' Grandad said, as if she wasn't almost fourteen but still five.

'For my *chemo*, dafty.'

'Ah, that. Suppose it's better down a tube than having to drink the stuff. Tastes like dandelion and durdock, apparently. You'd hate it. Which arm?'

It wasn't in her arm. The end of it, or the beginning of it, she couldn't decide which, was in her chest, burrowed under the skin near her collarbone. It stopped above her heart. The rest of it coiled like a tiny snake under a dressing, then out to hang between her and the drip stand.

'Jackson's got one as well,' Megan said. 'It's a central line or something.'

Grandad sounded impressed. *'Central line,'* Mrs Lemon was informed. 'Means you can use both hands for doing your hair and your nails with. You girls! Always fussing with your hair.'

He laughed. Megan laughed. He was trying to cheer her up, and she wanted him to think that he had succeeded. Grandad began to cough, which signalled that this had been a long phone call and his voice was tired, or he was just gripping the phone, the way he always did, had worn out his fingers.

'There now,' he said, when the coughing stopped, 'best be going, Pet Lamb. Kiss, night-night,' as if she was little again.

'Kiss, night-night,' Megan said, feeling as little as anything.

She waited for him to put down the phone.

No point in spoiling things. Best not to tell him that her hair might fall out with the chemo, that one day she might be as bald as Jackson.

Three

Good guys versus bad guys. Chemo versus Cancer. All happening in her veins and arteries, all heading off for that place in her head where things had gone wrong. Megan wondered if Good always won over Bad, the way it did in films and fairy stories.

It was late; it was dark. She should have been asleep. Instead, she lay listening to the hospital, the noises from the ward, the sounds from outside, the baby who seemed to have cried on and off for hours in a room further down the corridor.

Night-time was all so different.

Her door was half open. Megan didn't want to be shut out of everything that was going on, preferring the wedge of pale light which leaned in and took the edge off the darkness.

The nurses' voices were subdued, yet they still seemed to sing out, with nothing to mask them, no everyday bustle. There was hardly anyone about, no trolleys, no wheelchairs, no toddlers trying to escape.

The ring of phones haunted the place.

An odd shuffling footfall outside her room made Megan struggle up to see who it was. A parent in slippers and dressing gown was making her weary way along. Half an hour later, the steps returned, hesitating outside her door.

The woman looked in. 'Y'all right, love? Need a nurse or summat?' The kindness in her voice made Megan swallow, made her feel more lonely than ever.

'No, thank you.'

'Fust night on ward, is it?'

'Yes.'

'Never mind, you'll be right. Shall I get you a cup of cocoa or summat, help you go over? Just had one myself. These places weren't meant to help you sleep.' She gave a tight little laugh.

'I'm fine,' Megan said. 'Thanks, anyway.'

'Kipper's my little girl, by the way.' The woman paused, as if about to say something else, but thought better of it. 'All right, love. Nighty-night.'

'Excuse me,' Megan called out.

'Yes, love?'

'Is it her real name? Kipper?'

Another pause. 'No, but it's what she calls herself.

Ever since she got ill. Don't ask me why. And I'm not allowed to tell anyone her real name.'

'I like it,' Megan said, wondering if changing your name made it all feel better.

'Aye, well. It's what she wants while she's stuck here. Anything that helps, you know. Right. Best let you get some shut-eye. If you can. Night, love.' Off she went, her footsteps fading away until they were just whispers along the corridor.

When she heard the noise, Megan couldn't quite believe it. A cat? Outside? What was it doing all the way up there? A horrifying thought struck her. Perhaps it had climbed the walls and was on a ledge, unable to move with fright. It might need rescuing. She slid out of bed, heading for the window, but something tugged hard at her skin.

'Ouch, stupid thing.' Megan grabbed hold of her drip stand, patting down the dressing that held everything in place. Nothing had shifted, the line was still there, but the tape had lifted slightly. 'Fancy forgetting you.'

She gently drew back the curtains to look out, not wanting to frighten the cat should it, by some strange chance, be sitting right outside.

It wasn't. How could it be, twelve floors up and no windowsills?

But where was it?

Megan looked at a dull black sky with no stars, just

a faint suggestion of clouds, a sharper black, scattered like litter across it. Below was a collection of curious shapes, made almost sinister by the lamps, with gauzy skirts of light dropping into the darkness.

They were the roofs of the old buildings with their chimneys and ridges, gutters and piping; the oldest part of the hospital. Any number of cats could be living there.

They'd walked past these buildings in daylight, her and Mum and Dad, on that day they told her she had cancer. They seemed ordinary then. Red-brick walls. Grey slate roofs. Chimneys. Towers.

There were trees growing out of small patches of grass, wooden benches for people to sit in the sun. There had been patients out in their dressing gowns doing just that. And smoking, some of them, which was a bit daft, ill people smoking.

She didn't notice anything much the next time she came to hospital, just headed for St Peregrine's, named after the patron saint of cancer patients. That's what it said on the brochure, anyway.

The wing was a shining, glassy tower built on the side of the old Outpatients Department. Its windows glinted in the sunshine. You couldn't see inside.

Standing at her window now, Megan thought of Rapunzel. They did a play about her at school once, an alternative version *with attitude* according to the drama teacher. There was still a tower, made out of scaffolding, from which Rapunzel, Rapunzel had to let down her hair. There was still a prince to rescue her. Megan had been behind the scenes. The hair had to tumble from top to bottom. They made it out of yellow wool. Hundreds of strands of it, each strand twice the length of a man, all made into a wig for the girl who was playing the lead role. Megan ran her hands through her own hair and wondered how long it would last and if she'd ever be able to let it down from the top of a tower.

'What're you doing?'

Megan snapped the curtains closed, feeling a fool, thinking about fairytales and cats twelve floors up. 'Nothing.'

Jackson was silhouetted in the light from the corridor. 'You weren't climbing out, were you? It's easier to go through the door, catch the lift. That's how I do it. I can tell you the door code.'

Megan resented the tone, like a smirk, in his voice. Jackson who knew everything about anything. But he didn't know a thing about her and never would. 'I wasn't climbing out.'

'Good. Can I come in?' He was already in. 'If I stand out there, they'll catch me.' They should catch him, lock him in his room, stop him bothering people. 'Want the door closed?'

'No.'

'Suit yourself. What *were* you doing?'

'Are you always so nosy?' It was one of those questions which didn't need answering. 'I heard a cat. At least, I think it was a cat.' It all sounded pretty daft now. She expected him to laugh.

'That'll be Mr Henry. He's the moggy round here.'

'Ha-ha.'

'Keeps the rats down.' Jackson sat in the chair without waiting to be asked. There was a soft sigh as he sank into it. 'You get them as big as dogs in this place.'

'Big as dogs? I don't think so.' Nevertheless, Megan shifted a glance at the window and climbed back on to her bed, toes tingling at the thought.

'We're only metres away from a rat, you know, every single one of us in the whole wide world.'

In the dark room, he was just a solid, featureless shape, though it was a shape which moved constantly. His feet slid about on the floor, his fingers tapped the arms of the chair, as if he was made entirely of tightly wound springs, or had swallowed a whole tub of E-numbers and additives.

'But *we're* on the twelfth floor,' Megan reminded him.

'Well, maybe not *here*, exactly.' A small laugh. 'But on the ground, they're under us, gnawing away at the pipes and the walls. They eat anything. One day it's all going to collapse like an old mine and they'll be there clapping their tiny little hands, ready to chew on our bones. Not that they have hands. Not really. They have . . .'

42

'You're a complete nutter, do you know that?'

There was another laugh from Jackson, then silence, but for the thrum of his fingers on the wood of the chair. 'Mr Henry's been with this hospital since it was built.'

'So?'

'Since the *old* bit of the hospital was built . . . and you know what that means . . .' His words were a whisper, slow, menacing.

'No, but you're going to tell me, anyway.' Megan tried to make out his face in the dark, but all she could see were his eyes, gleaming. She yawned dramatically, pushed herself into bed and pulled the covers right up to her neck.

'Well . . . all *those* buildings must be hundreds of years old . . .'

'Not listening,' Megan said, sleepy now. 'Can't be bothered. If Mr Henry's been around that long, then he can keep for another day. Tell Becky and Laura, they'll like a spooky little cat story – you could call it *The Ghoooost of Mister Henry.*'

Jackson shifted in the chair. 'That's the chemo,' he said.

'What is?'

'Making you scabby to anyone who's trying to be nice to you. Making you laugh at things you shouldn't.'

'Like a ghost cat? Yeah, right.'

Jackson didn't reply.

Hah! She had him at last! Megan wished she could see the expression on his face, but just as quickly was glad that it was dark. Maybe he believed in things like that. Maybe she'd upset him. No. Not him. It was all just a joke, wasn't it? Just stupid stuff?

But the silence was like a wall between her and Jackson.

The door eased open. A nurse stood there for a moment, then switched on the light. The room swam with brightness. Megan screwed her eyes shut for a second.

'So this is where you are, Jackson,' the nurse said. She was small and mousy, with darting eyes, as if she was being hunted by someone, something. Mr Henry, perhaps. The thought made Megan want to smile, it made her suck in her cheeks, bite down on them. 'I've been looking all over for you. It's very late. You should be in your own room, not wandering the corridors. It sets a bad example to the little ones.'

'Just been keeping her company. She's new, you know,' Jackson said.

'I didn't invite him in. He just turned up,' Megan said. 'He keeps doing that.'

'Yes, I know,' the nurse replied, her voice knife-sharp, 'but call one of us if he bothers you. That's what this is for.' She indicated the bell push by the bed. 'Well, you'll know next time. As for you, Jackson, if you're still here in five minutes, it's going down in your notes and there'll be trouble. We'll tag you or something and there'll be no more walkabouts. We might even be forced to tie you to your bed.' Her mouth twisted into a kind of smile.

Jackson stood up. 'OK, I'm going.'

'Mind you do.' The nurse disappeared with a rattle of keys and a squeak of shoes on the floor.

'Thanks, Jackson. That's us both in trouble.'

He was by the door. 'Ignore her. She's always on my case.' Well, what a surprise. 'Want the light off? Or have I made you scared of rats and cats and things that go bump in the night?'

Megan shook her head. 'No to both questions.'

'See you, then.' Jackson left, the corridor swallowing him up in its shadows. Megan watched, trying to breathe normally, but her breath wouldn't come except in short gasps, as if she'd run a race, as if Jackson had worn her out just by being there.

Sure that he was gone and not coming back, Megan lay back in bed, but it wasn't comfortable. At last, she punched the top pillow, which gave a surprised wheeze, then she eased back on it, staring up at the ceiling where the light gleamed coldly back at her. Somewhere, out on the ward, the baby began to cry once more, bleating like a lost lamb.

Four

Sleep came in snatches, like small rafts floating by. Every now and then, Megan climbed on to one and began to settle. Yet, just as her body relaxed, her breathing slowed and everything felt comfortable, something disturbed her, a pull on her drip, a sound from outside, a rush of thoughts, and the raft just sailed from under her.

When morning came, with its own brand of noise – the rumble of the medicine trolley, the chatter of breakfast plates, the emerging busyness of the place – it was almost a relief not to have to think about sleep.

Megan climbed out of bed to clean her teeth, but that simple task made her so tired she couldn't bear the thought of trying to shower with the stupid drip attached to her or attempting to get dressed. She looked in the mirror and was dismayed at how pale her face was, how dark her eyes were, as if someone had tried to erase them with a dirty old rubber. And her lips were so dry. Where was her tin of vaseline?

When Jackson arrived he looked great, as if nothing affected him.

'So they didn't tie you up, then? Didn't tag you?' Megan said, getting back into bed, which felt so much more inviting than it had during the night.

'Nah. They like having someone to complain about.' He grinned at her. 'Any sign of the cat?'

'No.' Megan yawned, not believing there'd ever been a cat, a Mr Henry, from the eighteen hundreds or whenever. She'd imagined the whole thing, that's what it was. Maybe it was the chemo making her hear things.

Jackson settled into her room as if he owned the place. If he thought he could just turn up every time he liked, then he had another think coming. And just how was he so . . . cheerful all the time, so full of energy?

From outside her room came a noise rather like a large but muffled hairdryer. It was coming nearer and nearer.

'What's that?'

'The buffer,' Jackson answered. 'They polish the floors with it. It's got a brush and it spins round. Like one of those street cleaners. They won't let me have a try on it, but I know where they keep them. All I need is the code to open the door . . .'

She should never have asked.

'Do you want me to go?' Jackson smiled at her. 'I won't talk too much, nothing about cats or rats. Promise. When your friends appear, I'm out of here. But while you're waiting . . . can I stay?' Megan tried to speak. Jackson just carried on. 'What else are you going to do? Stare at walls?'

'Draw. I like to draw. People.' Megan gazed down at her hands, afraid that he might be right about her friends after all; that they wouldn't come. But this was only the second day. There was time. And Gemma was texting her, sending rows of ☺s to make her feel better, let her know she wasn't forgotten. The Twins wanted to know if there was anyone nice to look at.

'You need peace and quiet to draw,' Megan said, giving him a pointed look. 'I do, anyway.' Her sketch pad, a present from Grandad, was still empty, the new pencils still unused, still in the packet, but *he* didn't need to know that.

'I haven't spoken for at least five seconds,' Jackson said. 'I'm waiting to hear all about you. Or I can tell you all about me. You've met my mum.' He made a face. 'I've met yours. But there's probably a lot more where they came from.' Jackson pulled another face. 'There's hundreds in my family.'

Megan thought about hers. What was there to tell? It was so small. Everyone had got married late, is all she knew. Like missing a bus and catching the next one, or even the one after that. Grandad was past fifty when Mum was born, past eighty when *she* was born. Dad had one brother who had a wife and one son. The sum total of her family could be squeezed into one house and still leave room.

'We don't have to speak at all, if you don't want to,' Jackson said, twiddling his thumbs, shifting around in the chair. He was grinning like a maniac. 'I'll just sit here and think of when I get out. Don't mind me. No need to say a word.' Pulling down his hat, he stretched out in the chair as if about to go to sleep, the way parrots do when you cover their cages. 'I'll just wait for *you* to say something.' He was watching Megan from under the brim of the hat, with that grin still on his face, his long legs twitching, feet tapping as if he was listening to music.

'Jackson! Do you never just sit still?'

'Me? No.' Jackson smiled. 'It's the music, see? They say I take after my great-grandfather.' He pushed his hat up a fraction. 'You want to hear about him?'

'No.'

'This is his trilby . . .'

Megan made an exaggerated sigh.

The hat was pulled back down, but Jackson's whole body still pulsed with rhythm, as if it ran right through his blood, like chemotherapy.

'All *right*!' Megan folded her arms and refused to

look at him any more. He was so . . . She rolled her eyes . . . what was he, exactly? 'Where do you live? Tell me *that*.'

Jackson shook his head. 'Nah. Too late. You had your chance and blew it.'

From outside the open door came a familiar sound, giggly and high-pitched.

'Hello,' Megan said, her voice flat.

Two heads appeared. 'We're looking for Jackson.'

The girl called Laura was the first to speak. Becky gave her a nudge, as if she alone owned Jackson, as if only she had the right to enquire about him as it was *her* brother they were visiting.

'Yes,' Becky added, 'we want to ask him Something Important.'

'He's here,' Megan answered. There was an eruption of giggles.

'*He's in her room* . . .' an astonished voice squeaked.

The two girls inched through the doorway, both wearing jeans and T-shirts, glittery slides in their hair, flashing trainers. They might have been sisters rather than friends, might have been dressed by the same mother, from the same wardrobe. They each wore a rucksack, one shocking pink, the other powder blue. Megan couldn't stop herself smiling. Had she ever been like this? She glanced at Jackson as if to say, *You deal with them*, and busied herself looking for her tin of vaseline, opening the small side doors of her locker and there it was. She took it out, opened it and began to spread some on to her lips.

Jackson swivelled round in the chair in that lazy way of his. 'Hi, you two! Come to see your brother, Becky?'

'Yes.'

'That's good. How is he, anyway?'

Something flashed across the girl's face, a moment of doubt, indecision. Perhaps she didn't really know. 'He might be coming home soon. Tomorrow, maybe.'

Laura rolled her eyes. 'She always says tomorrow, and he never does.'

Becky scowled.

'And is he waiting to see you?' Jackson said.

Becky nodded and exchanged a glance with Laura, seeming to come to some sort of silent understanding. They both turned to Jackson. With one voice the girls asked, 'Are you going to be her boyfriend?' They glanced meaningfully at Megan, who felt her face flush.

'Hey, girls!' Jackson replied, his face serious. They frowned. 'The name is Megan, not *her*. Say hello . . .'

'Hi, Megan,' the girls chimed obediently, then turned to gaze at him once more. Despite everything, Megan found herself gazing too, taking in the whole relief of his face, from his long eyelashes to his full mouth – everything about him carved out like a statue, only walking, talking, smiling.

'And I hardly know Megan,' Jackson went on. 'She

hardly knows me, as she's only been here a day and well, you wouldn't want me to rush things now, would you? Rushing's not good.' The girls glowed with all the attention and stood in the doorway, eyes like owls. 'Except when you need to rush to see your brother, Becky. Who's been *waiting* to see his sister.'

Another look between the girls which seemed to say, *Yes, it's time to go*, and they made to turn back. Yet, obviously, they weren't finished.

'Put your spooky face on, Jackson,' Becky said. 'Laura hasn't seen it.'

Jackson shook his head.

'Pleeease,' begged Laura.

'Spooky face, spooky face,' they chanted.

Megan tried not to laugh.

'OK, but then you have to go,' Jackson said. 'Close your eyes.' The girls closed their eyes. Jackson beamed a smile at Megan then pulled a face like a grotesque mask. 'O . . . p . . . en your eyesssss, girls . . .'

Becky and Laura did as he commanded and squealed, throwing their hands to their faces, hiding their eyes but for the gaps between their fingers. The mask fell and Jackson was back. The girls stopped squealing, laughter beginning to bubble up instead.

'Now go,' ordered Jackson with a grin. 'Go on. Scat.'

'See you later, Jackson. See you later, *Megan*.' Off they went in a storm of giggles.

Megan replaced the lid of her vaseline, pushing it back into her locker, and tidying as she went along, determined not to look at Jackson. He just loved being the centre of attention, obviously. She wasn't going to be stupid about him, like everyone else.

'So . . . what?' There was a grin in his voice.

Why did he always sound like he was laughing at her?

'They're like your own little fan club.' Megan continued tidying. 'You should give out badges. Mugs with *Jackson* all over them. Hats. You could sell them.'

Jackson began rifling through his pockets, then stopped. 'And I thought I had badges in here. You could have had one for nothing, now that we're almost going out and everything.' His eyes were huge, shining. Megan tried not to look at him any more, her cheeks warm. 'I mean, give it another few days, we'll be engaged, if Laura and Becky have anything to do with it.'

Megan gaped at him, feeling her whole body blush. 'Very funny, Jackson. So funny I could laugh myself to bits.' But Megan couldn't laugh, even if she'd wanted to. Tiredness was flooding over her, like some huge wave. She closed her eyes. If Jackson wanted to be part of a story made up by two little girls, then let him. No way was she joining in. And if she kept her eyes shut, maybe he'd get the hint.

'Right, sleepyhead, I'm going.'

'OK,' Megan muttered.

'Off, right now.'

She kept her eyes clamped shut. 'So you keep saying . . .'

'By the way . . .'

If only she had something she could throw at him. Something sharp. Or heavy. That would do. Only right then she didn't have the energy, even if she had a whole line of things to chuck at him.

'What?'

'Vaseline.' Leaning forward, Jackson touched her mouth, so gently that it might have been something delicate, something that might break. He dabbed at her bottom lip, concentrating so hard that this might have been the most important task ever. 'You missed a bit,' he said.

Megan couldn't speak. He was so close to her that she couldn't utter a word, so close she could hardly breathe. For that brief moment everything seemed to stop, as if the whole world, their world, on the ward, in the hospital, was put on hold and dared not move, because if it did, the moment might disappear.

At last, Jackson's gaze met hers. There was no smile in his eyes, no mockery; just the window, opposite, the shape of it, mirroring in each one, perfect reflections of the day's pale light.

Five

It was a silly game, one to be played when you're lying in a hospital bed, not one that Gemma or the Twins would appreciate. It wasn't like football with all of its rules and its time limits, or going out looking at boys in the shopping centre. There were no winners, no losers. It was more like Patience, that card game Grandad liked to play on his own.

All you had to do was close your eyes and listen, try to work out whose footsteps were going past the door, or who was laughing, or talking. You couldn't cheat by opening your eyes. Not that anyone would know. You could make it as complicated or as simple as you liked, depending on how much time you had, or how bored or sick you were feeling.

There was too much time.

She was bored for most of it.

And now she was feeling sick.

Sister Brewster's shoes squeaked. Megan had studied this. Siobhan's shoes had a kind of clicky sound. It seemed to come from the heels. The cancer consultant, Frog-Man, dragged his feet as if he couldn't lift them properly, or liked the sound they made, liked everyone to know who was walking past their door. Or maybe his job was too hard. Maybe it made his shoes heavier.

He had a huge laugh, which he must have kept for the ward, or maybe just the little ones. You could always hear him. Like everything was a joke. Like this wasn't a ward full of cancer patients trying to dodge *the bigger thing*.

The bigger thing.

When they first told her she had cancer and would need to go into hospital, Megan just sat waiting for the words she'd just heard to go away, so that she wouldn't have to think about it.

'What if I say no,' she said, because they refused to go away. 'What if I don't want to go to hospital?'

Mum and Dad had looked at her as if she'd stripped off all her clothes in front of a bus queue.

'Well, Megan,' Frog-Man said, 'it's a big thing, this. An important thing. The cancer, the treatment. If you don't have the treatment, and let the cancer stay, you could die. And that's a bigger thing altogether.' He made a tent of his hands and twirled his thumbs round each other. 'It's about trying to help you dodge the bigger thing.'

Mum had cried then. She'd obviously been trying hard not to break down in front of Megan and make things seem much worse than they were, but after Frog-Man's summing up of the situation, she must have thought they couldn't get any worse at all.

Dad just sat there like a blank piece of paper on a noticeboard.

Megan knew she was beaten.

It was like going to the seaside and putting every last penny into that stupid machine where the best prize never gets pushed to the front. Every last penny. And wishing you had more to shove in and make it come to you. Only you stop there, because otherwise, it's just mad. You had to know when you were beaten – at the Amusements and in a cancer specialist's office.

'OK, then,' she said, gazing back into Frog-Man's eyes, trying hard not to cry, or shake, taking it on the chin. As Grandad would say.

Sister Brewster was coming down the corridor and talking to Jackson in a brisk sort of way, sounding like a teacher with a naughty boy. There seemed to be a lot of that. Somehow or other he was always in trouble, and always being caught out. Which meant he wasn't very good at it. Something about that made Megan smile, even though she was feeling absolutely rotten.

They weren't wrong when they said she might feel unwell with the chemo.

'So there's this phone call, Jackson, telling me that you're all the way down near X-ray. Correct me if I'm wrong, but you weren't down for an X-ray this afternoon, were you?'

'Not exactly.'

'*Not exactly*. And as far as I'm aware you aren't due an X-ray at all.' There was a pause when, no doubt, Sister Brewster would be giving him one of her looks. 'Jackson, you know how important it is that we have just a tiny clue about where you are. I had Kipper trying to get off the ward too. You know she watches you like a hawk.'

Sometimes Megan wished she could get off the ward. Even if it was with Jackson, even if it meant admitting she wouldn't know where to go and having to follow him around.

But Jackson seemed to prefer to disappear on his own. Megan never quite knew if he was on the ward, or had gone home, or was just wandering about the hospital. For all his chattering, he didn't tell her very much.

'Someone phoned you to say where I was,' Jackson was telling Sister Brewster. 'No need to get so stressed. It's not like I hopped on the 47 bus or anything.'

'Jackson . . .'

He'd be standing there, brazening it out, as if he

liked getting into trouble. They were past her room now, their voices less clear. It was no wonder Jackson wanted to escape to other places, to a change of scenery, no wonder he went walkabout. This hospital, this room, these walls and corridors, were it, were all there was, just as he'd said.

At least the little ones had a playroom. They even had a play specialist who let them mess about with toys and paints and clay. There were finger puppets and dressing-up clothes. If you were little, you could pretend to be a doctor or a nurse and stick needles in your doll.

Siobhan said it was to help children feel normal, to stop them thinking about bad things, to prepare them for all the tests. If they had some idea, it wasn't so frightening for them.

'It's all right for you older ones,' she said. 'You can understand what's happening. But the radiotherapy machines, they're like some huge great monster when you're a little person. It's only for a few minutes, but it's like an eternity to the wee ones.'

You didn't have to be little to feel time dragging. Being stuck here was like an eternity. Too tired to move, not enough energy to draw, too wiped out to even text her friends. Not that she wanted to. What was there to tell? They were at school doing real stuff. She was here doing nothing, just listening to Jackson getting himself into trouble.

They wouldn't understand.

She couldn't even remember what she'd be doing now if she *was* at school. She couldn't picture any of it. It was all outside the walls and she was inside. Like being trapped in a snow globe without the snow.

Megan blinked open her eyes. She hadn't really been sleeping but it was easier to lie with her eyes closed than keep them open. She'd managed to draw some useless scribbles earlier, but it was as if the chemo had stopped her mind from working properly and her hand from drawing anything good. She tried to read her book. It was a great book. At least it had been when she started it at home. There was course-work she could be doing too. They'd sorted some out for her at school and Mum brought it in earlier, stowing it in her locker. She must have noticed the Don't-Even-Think-I'm-Doing-Homework sort of look Megan gave her, so didn't mention it. Besides, there were cards to put up on the wall behind the bed. Mum read out all of the names and all of the messages, every single one of them, so that the words spun around in Megan's head.

It was a relief when Mum decided she had to post off a parcel to Dad and though, once she'd gone, there was still the busyness of the ward outside her door, there was peace in her room.

For a little while at least.

Now there was someone at her door.

Megan turned to see an alien standing there, or a princess. She wasn't quite sure. A head as smooth as an egg. Big blue eyes. No eyebrows. And thin as a pencil. The pink frilly dress skimmed her shoulders and fell like a lacy sack around her. She had a fine tube coming from her nose and taped to her cheek. Her name bracelet looked two sizes too big. She was the most beautiful thing Megan had ever seen.

'Hello . . . are you . . . Kipper?' The alien nodded. Megan pulled herself to a half-sitting position and her book slid to the floor. 'Are you looking for Jackson?'

A shake of the head.

'I was talking to your mum the other night.' Was it last night? Or the night before? She couldn't remember. Not that it mattered. The girl didn't say anything.

Megan wondered what she was doing there in her doorway and hoped that someone would come and take her away again. She shook herself. How horrible can you get? Did the chemo really make you that nasty?

'Is there something wrong? Will I call for a nurse?' Kipper shook her head at every question. Megan was tired out. 'Well, d'you want to come in?'

Interest. At last.

'Jackson never bothers to ask, so you needn't.' Megan smiled, but the girl didn't smile back or show signs of moving any time soon. She stood like a wedge in the door.

'So, how long have you been in?'

Kipper shrugged. She was looking at Megan with a kind of expectance on her face. What did she want? Why was she here?

'Are you allowed juice or anything? Or sweets. I've got loads.' Was she meant to offer her stuff, or let her drink from her glass? Too late now.

No reply.

Kipper began to gaze around the room, as if checking that everything was in its right place, or trying to remember something. Perhaps she'd been in there once and wanted to have a look, now that someone else was in it.

'D'you like it here?' Megan said. 'Probably not. Home's best, isn't it?'

Kipper was staring at her, listening perhaps, but showing no sign of understanding.

'But if you have to be here, the nurses are nice, aren't they? I like Siobhan. She's funny. And the doctors are all right. They just ask too many questions.' Megan tried to laugh, but the girl looking at her like that seemed to suck out all her energy.

'Have you been in long? I haven't but I'm fed up already. Do you get bored? I think if they gave me some maths to do, I'd just do it, I'm that bored.' Megan gave her a great big grin. She felt like a clown with a painted-on smile, there to make little children laugh. 'And this chemo makes you feel rubbish, doesn't it?'

The girl looked at her as if she'd gone a bit mad and that clown smiles were for babies.

'So, you're nearly seven?'

Kipper nodded, gave one final look around the room and drifted away.

'Bye, then,' Megan said into the space she'd left behind.

They said she might feel sick after a day or so, but Megan didn't realise how tired she would feel too. Nothing made it any better. Lying back on the pillows didn't help; turning on her side was no good. She had just closed her eyes in complete misery when she heard Jackson at her door. His sandals made a soft scraping when he walked.

Great.

Jackson crashed his drip stand into the chair leg. 'Whoops, sorry. I keep colliding into things with this. Can I come in? I'm keeping out of Rooster's way.'

No, Megan wanted to scream. *I don't want company, I want to vomit!* She threw up into her bowl.

'Brilliant!' Jackson was leaning against the wall, grinning at her. 'You've gone green.' Slumping into the pillows, Megan wiped her mouth on the back of her hand. 'I don't do green when I'm sick.' Jackson gave her a big smile, teeth white against his black skin. 'It's more like grey.'

Megan closed her eyes, wishing he would go. Then

something occurred to her. Jackson was breathless, as if he'd run a race. She forced open her eyes once more and looked at him. He was sitting upright in the chair next to her bed. He didn't look comfortable. She saw his chest move in and out, his shoulders rise and fall, saw the bloom of moisture on his skin.

'Are you OK?'

Jackson smiled at her. 'Been to X-ray and back, that's all. Long way.'

It took some time to get his breath, but at last he relaxed back into the chair, stretched out his legs and was the old Jackson again.

'Meet Great-grandfather Dawes,' he said, pointing at his T-shirt. It was long and baggy. On the front was a big picture of an old man in a hat, playing a trumpet.

'Jackson T. Dawes. Named me after him cos the day I was born, I came out dancing and singing instead of screaming.'

'Yeah. And you haven't stopped.'

Jackson began to laugh. This was the first time Megan had heard it, a surprisingly low laugh, deep and husky, right from his stomach, which made his shoulders dance. It made him seem an awful lot older than he was and it made her laugh too, no matter how tired she was.

'So . . . you want me to do your hair for you?'

Megan took a deep breath as another wave of sickness flooded over her. 'Stop messing about, Jackson.'

66

'It's probably going to fall out, anyway. Might as well shave it off.'

Another deep breath, trying to keep her stomach from heaving, not wanting to be sick, not wanting to be reminded about her hair. 'Oh, this is so yucky.'

'Yeah, it is. But it'll get better. Honest. What have you got? You never told me.' Flitting from subject to subject, from flower to flower, like an insect, a bee, a butterfly. Megan turned her head, refusing to answer. Jackson carried on. 'Mine's so rare it hasn't got a name. They're writing books about it. Bet yours has a name.'

Megan closed her eyes once more. 'Medulla ... thingummy ... something. I don't know.' She glanced back at him. 'Are you going away soon? Please say you are.'

Jackson shrugged, grinned again, then gripped the arms of the chair, pushing himself up from the seat, as if it were just a bit too far, a bit too hard. Megan gazed at the muscles on his arms, the sinews showing through his skin, the tiny pearls of sweat.

'D'you need anything?' he said.

'Jackson ...' Sister Brewster was at the door, carrying a kidney-shaped dish and a medication chart. She laid them both on the bed table.

Megan sighed. What were they going to do to her now?

'What she *needs* is for you to go,' Sister Brewster said. 'Hop it. Now.'

'OK, OK. Just getting to know each other,' Jackson said, pushing his drip stand ahead of him. 'You told us to, remember?'

Sister Brewster raised her eyebrows and indicated the open door with a nod of her head. There was a slight twitch at the corner of her mouth, as if she was trying not to laugh, trying hard to keep a stern face.

Megan might have laughed herself, but for one thing. 'Oh . . .' she wailed, scrabbling for the bowl in front of her. With one hand, she swept her hair out of the way, and with the other, held the vomit bowl beneath her chin. Just in time.

'Spectacular,' Jackson said.

Six

Kipper was sitting in the middle of Megan's bed, her lacy dress spread all around her like pink meringue. Megan tried not to look surprised when she came out of the bathroom. She just hung up her towel and put away her toilet bag. The girl sat motionless, like a statue, or some kind of wingless fairy for the top of a Christmas tree. Megan wasn't sure if she was allowed on someone else's bed. She wasn't sure if a nurse needed to know that Kipper was here. They might think she'd gone walkabout, done a Jackson.

'Hiya . . . I've been trying to have a shower, but it's not easy with this stupid thing.' She gave her drip stand a little kick. 'Did you have some supper?'

A tiny shake of the head.

'Me neither. It smells like . . .'

'Sweaty socks,' Kipper said.

Megan put some vaseline on her lips and slid the tin under her pillow. 'Exactly. And everything tastes like cardboard to me. Move over, I'm wrecked.' Kipper shuffled to one side. 'I need to have a sleep or at least a lie-down. This stuff makes you so tired! Have you had any yet?'

Kipper nodded.

'Did it make you tired?'

A look. Nothing more.

'Well, it's got me whacked out.'

There was a noise outside which made Kipper give a little start. It was just the porter. His footsteps were easy to recognise. He had a limp, so that one foot trailed just a little behind the other but the biggest clue was the noise made by the wheels of the supper trolley he delivered. He brought it to the ward at half past five; it was plugged into a socket on the wall to keep the meals warm, and a couple of hours later he took it away again.

'Will we get into trouble for not eating our meals, do you think? I'm new, so I don't really know.' Another shrug. 'I think a cat's got your tongue.'

A flicker of a smile. 'Mr Henry.'

Megan nodded. 'Ah-ha! I thought so. Have you seen him?' The little girl shook her head. 'I think I heard him, but I'm not sure. Jackson said it was him. But I don't know how it could be. Do you? Not all the way up here. What's a cat doing all the way up here? I mean, how could a cat climb so high? That's what I'd like to know.'

'Brian runs up our tree,' Kipper said, her voice quiet. 'Then the fire brigade comes to get him down again.'

Megan laughed, but just as quickly she stopped. Kipper's face had crumpled and tears began to pool in her eyes, as if the whole world had collapsed around her, like a lost child in a disaster zone.

'Oh, what's the matter? Come here.' She put her arm around the little girl, who nudged close to her. Her hands were cold on Megan's, her fingers light as feathers, as if they belonged to a younger child or a tiny bird. Megan pulled the covers over the girl, tucking them around her. 'Is that better?'

Kipper nodded.

'Is Brian your cat?'

'He's a kitten.'

'Who's looking after him while you're here?'

Kipper sniffed and snuggled in a little nearer, so that Megan could feel every angle of the girl's body next to hers and the smooth bald head burrowed under her chin. It felt remarkably warm and not quite bald, but slightly downy, like a baby's. 'Grandma and Grandad're looking after him.'

'Well, that's good, isn't it?'

Kipper didn't answer. She just curled up around Megan, arms and legs trapping her in a fierce hug, and began to cry so hard that her body shook as if some invisible hand had mistaken her for a cloth and was shaking the dust out of her.

Megan woke with a start and had no idea of the time or where she was. Everything seemed stuck together in a damp sweaty mess and she couldn't think why. When she tried to move, there was the reason, still clamped around her, fast asleep. Kipper took a long, shuddery breath as if rebelling against being woken, though she didn't wake at all, just shifted position, stretched and settled down again, aware of nothing.

Her face looked quite relaxed now, as if all her worries had been forgotten, as if there was nothing going on at all in her head. A deep, dreamless, worry-less sleep.

Worries.

How come Kipper had worries when she was so young?

Kipper shifted slightly as if she knew she was under scrutiny. Her feet slid into view, slippers still on. Pink. Sparkly. What noise would they make? Would they do a kind of pitter-patter, or a slide? They looked slightly big. Maybe they'd slip a bit, and drag along the floor.

Not drag. The slippers were too pretty to drag, the girl too light, too delicate.

Megan studied her. She was still partially cocooned in bedding. One cheek was pale as milk but the other, which had been clamped to Megan's collarbone but was now only half resting there, had furrows imprinted on it and glistened pinkly. A pixie ear, whose whorls and tiny ridges looked almost transparent and delicate as a flower, reminded her of the little girl she used to babysit for. Mr and Mrs Baker's daughter from Number 19. She was only two and a half. Did ears grow at the same pace as the rest of you?

Kipper was nearly seven.

'Oh,' Megan said to the air, conscious now of her arm wrapped around the girl. 'What am I going to do with you?'

As if in answer Jackson appeared at the door, took one look and grinned. 'Have you kidnapped her or has she kidnapped you?'

Megan shook her head. 'I'm not really sure.'

Jackson sat on the edge of the bed and leaned into Kipper. 'She's not waking up any time soon. That's for sure. You're stuck there. For ever, possibly.'

'Yeah, but my arm's gone numb.'

'Uh-oh, we'll have to shift her.'

Jackson slid the covers off her and somehow peeled Kipper away from Megan, who immediately felt the cold. She pulled her dressing gown from the head of the bed and wrapped it around the sleeping girl, who was now lying between them on the bed.

Blood pumped back down Megan's arm. She flexed her fingers then eased her head from side to side, realising how much her neck was aching.

'What time is it?' she asked.

'Day staff're going home soon.'

So she hadn't been asleep for very long. Yet it felt like hours.

Siobhan came in then. 'Ah. Here she is. Her mammy goes off to the café for a bit of a break and she comes back to an empty bed!'

'I think she's missing her kitten. Worried about him,' Megan explained.

'Is she?'

'And I didn't know what to do. Or if she was allowed or anything. In my room, I mean. But she was too upset to send her away. Then she fell asleep.'

'Poor wee mite. I'll take her back.'

Megan watched Siobhan lift the girl in such a swift yet delicate movement, so carefully, that she might have been something fragile or precious, made out of thin pink glass, something which might shatter if you just breathed the wrong way.

Kipper, however, still heavily asleep, nestled herself into the nurse's body, as if she believed that no such disaster could possibly happen to her.

It was past eleven and she should have been asleep, but Megan's mind wouldn't stop working. She tried reading again, she tried drawing, she tried lying as still as possible, hoping that sleep would come, but it didn't. Eventually she climbed out of bed and headed off down the corridor.

The visitors' waiting room was dark, except for a

dull silver glow from outside, and from the corner table, an anglepoise lamp oozing out a small pool of golden light. Megan was drawn in when she had intended only to take a walk. It seemed cosy, somehow, peaceful.

Negotiating the chairs and coffee table with her drip stand, Megan made her way to the window and looked out at the river, the roads, the buildings, all alive with light, all so different at night. Everything stretched out from the hospital gates like a glittering blanket, spread over that other world, the one Mum lived in, the one she brought with her in little parcels of information – about next door's dog, or the church roof being stripped of its lead, or the new 'Sainsbury's Express' opening at last and how she'd gone to have a look. She might have been talking about a trip to Mars. But Megan had listened and tried to look interested, when all she wanted was for Mum to go. Which made her feel bad, ungrateful. Even now.

Megan switched off the lamp so that the room was almost completely dark. Somehow, that made her feel better, made her forget about Mum, made everything outside shine even brighter.

It was wide awake, the city. Strings of brightly lit roads lay in all directions, like some kind of strange crop in a black field. They reached far into the distance. Cars moved along in fits and starts. Who were they, all those people driving? Where were they going at this time of night?

From nearby, street lamps bled a hazy whiteness like netting, which caught the odd shadow; a person, an animal. Mr Henry, perhaps. If he really existed. He might be prowling the city, right now, looking for rats.

A train trundled across the bridge over the river and away. Megan wished she could be on it. A late-night bus eased along the road past the hospital. That would do, to take her home.

Above her roared an aeroplane. Whether it was coming in to land or taking off, she couldn't tell. Nobody on that aeroplane, no one in that world beneath her, in those cars, the train, the buses or the shadows, knew a thing about her. She was as insignificant as an ant, just someone in a window looking out. Someone whose friends hadn't come.

Two whole days.

It was school, Gemma said, when she texted; it was homework, the Twins said. It was all the other stuff they did, when not at school. And the hospital was so far away. When she came home, they said, they'd see her every day. It wouldn't be long . . . ☺ ☺ ☺ ☺ ☺

Jackson was right, and for that Megan wanted to hate him, but couldn't. He'd tried to warn her and she hadn't listened. And she was missing her friends the way Kipper was missing her kitten, so much it hurt.

The moon suddenly appeared in the window, from

behind a cloud. It looked like a ball of ice, illuminating the room with a light which made the anaemic walls more bloodless, more colourless, the line of blue chairs more shadowy somehow, their worn-down edges weary, raw, like wounds. Megan wiped her eyes. It was stupid to cry, but she couldn't help it.

A movement in the dark made her squeal.

'Ssshhhh!' Jackson said.

'Well, stop creeping up on people!'

'I'm not! This is *my* hiding place, you know.'

'Not tonight, it isn't,' Megan managed, 'and I'm not hiding.'

Jackson shuffled up to her. 'Are you going to at least share?'

Megan couldn't speak any more, not wanting to be crying in front of him, not wanting to be so weak, so stupid, but not able to stop any of it. And just like that she was thinking of Kipper again. Poor little alien princess.Why did she keep turning up? And changing her name? What was all that about? Yet, why not? Nothing was real in hospital. Not like home. Maybe changing your name made you feel better about being ill, being stuck on a ward. You could pretend it was happening to someone else.

If only she could change *her* name. Be someone else.

'Am I making you worse?' Jackson said, his voice soft. 'Do you want me to go?'

Megan looked up at him. She felt dwarfed, he was so tall. She barely reached his shoulder, yet there was something about his height which gave him a strength and steadiness, like a solid piece of rock, something that would never move or let you down.

No, she didn't want him to go.

'It's OK,' she said.

'So . . . what's up?'

'Don't know.'

Megan so wanted to lean her head against his arm, rest it there, just for a second or two. She did know. It was everything. It was the way he could be so happy and cheerful all the time, when she was so angry and upset. It was not believing what he said about her friends. When he was right all along. It was not wanting him around her. When, really, she needed him more than anything. Especially now.

'Hey,' Jackson moved closer. Their drip stands nudged into each other with a dull clunk. 'Don't worry, whatever it is.'

Then his arm was around her shoulders, warm as jumpers, pulling her in so close that she melted into the shape of him, so that in the sharpness of the moonlight, the jazzy glitter of the city and the strings of brightly lit roads, it was all just a blur. Megan couldn't see where she ended or where he began, but it didn't matter. Nothing mattered any more.

* * *

'Thank you,' Megan said later. Her eyes felt swollen and sore with so much crying.

'For what . . . ?'

'I don't know. Being here, I suppose.'

But it was more than that. It was everything else.

It was Jackson making her feel that it didn't matter if she cried. It was him making everything seem just that little bit more simple, that little bit less confusing. It was Jackson making her feel safe, there in the window, with the black sky all around her.

At last she moved away, gently shrugging off his arm from around her shoulders. 'We should get back, I suppose. Before they come and find us.'

'Let them. What're they going to do. Sack us? Send us home?' His face shone in the moonlight. He was smiling.

It was a nice smile, not one which laughed at her, for a change. Megan knew that Jackson was trying to be her friend, trying to help, when there was no Gemma to talk to, no Twins to make silly jokes about everything as if they understood what it was like to be in hospital, to have cancer.

Megan gave Jackson a watery smile.

He really was all she had. She'd have to be nice to him, stop treating him like he was in the way all the time. Jackson leaned in as if he knew all of this. Megan could feel his breath on her face, clean, toothpaste breath.

79

'Let's just stay here,' he whispered, as if that would solve everything.

But how could it?

'Where else can we go?' Megan said, surprising herself with the bitterness she felt all of a sudden. 'There's just this stupid ward, this stupid place.' The words came out in short bursts, as if Jackson was to blame for everything when clearly he wasn't.

Yet she couldn't help it.

The anger wouldn't go away. *Just staying here* meant she couldn't get away, but would be sucked into the hospital, into Jackson's world and end up like him, always in trouble, or like Kipper, upset about her cat.

She didn't want to be in trouble, didn't want to be upset. She wanted to be normal and away from here and not have cancer any more. It was rubbish. Everything. And Jackson *couldn't* help. No one could and there was no point in *just staying here*.

It was then that Jackson bent his face to hers and kissed her with the softest peck of his lips. Megan moved away. 'Don't.'

Jackson stood very still, as if paused by the press of a button. The air between them almost crackled. Megan couldn't tell if he was hurt, amused or angry. She could easily un-pause him, easily feel him close to her again through the thin material of her dressing gown, breathe in every breath he took. She could easily kiss him back.

But no.

It wasn't right. Nothing was.

The space between them grew bigger and deeper than a canyon. The air cooled.

'It's OK. I get it,' Jackson said.

'No! You don't get it! It's just . . .' The words wouldn't come. Megan felt even more hollow inside.

But didn't you have to feel at least a little bit happy to want to kiss someone?

Megan tried to make her way to the door, only now, in the dark, the furniture seemed bigger than before, her drip stand seemed to have grown more feet, more wheels. It kept colliding into things.

'Don't go,' Jackson said. 'Stay a bit longer. I'm sorry. Promise I won't try anything else.'

There was that grin in his voice once more, which said nothing had upset him. Nothing and no one, not even she, could ever really hurt him.

It made Megan smile, just a little bit, as if it was all a bad dream, all the upset she felt, and now she was awake.

Jackson began to fold himself down on to the low chairs lining the back wall.

'*What are you doing?*' Megan said.

'Sometimes I just lay me down to sleep.' He sounded like his mother or someone older even.

'On *those*?'

'Yeah. Try it.'

Megan slumped down on the row of seats opposite. They weren't uncomfortable, not really. She drew up her feet, wrapping her dressing gown around them like a blanket. She could fall asleep quite easily. Had Jackson ever done that? For the whole night? Had anyone ever caught him? She gazed at him as he stretched out like a cat in its basket.

'Jackson?' she whispered.

'Sssssh! I'm planning.'

Megan frowned. 'Planning what?' There was a chuckle in answer, nothing more. Oh no. Surely he wasn't aiming to go off the ward tonight? 'Are you going to escape again?'

No answer.

'You're going to drive them crazy, you know.'

Another chuckle, then silence. Obviously, Jackson didn't care about upsetting nurses or doctors, he didn't bother about rules and regulations, except to break them, to get away just for a little while.

If only she could do the same.

Megan wanted a place to go, just like Jackson, somewhere which wasn't her room, wasn't the ward, or the visitors' waiting area, or the place they called *School*, but which was just a table, a couple of chairs and a computer in the corner of the playroom.

'Where d'you really get to?' she said. 'When you go off the ward?'

Jackson propped himself up on his elbow. Megan could feel him watching her, as if he was trying to work her out. 'Well, it's a big hospital,' he said. 'Hundreds of floors, and buildings and lifts. Then there's the old bit, lots of corridors, and shadows and things you don't want to meet in dead of night . . .'

'Stop it, Jackson,' Megan warned. 'Keep that stuff for Becky and Laura. Come on. Out with it!'

There was a laugh from low in his throat. 'OK . . . well . . . the porters' place, staff restaurant, laundry, visitors' restaurant, chapel . . .' He paused as if for breath, or to see what she made of it so far.

Megan looked at Jackson, imagining him not stopping at the chapel, or the laundry, imagining him walking very casually, very coolly, out through the main doors, down the path, away into the street.

'. . . the doctors' residence, the nurses' home . . . at least I think that's what it was . . .'

'You haven't been to all those places.'

'I so have.'

'Why?'

'Why not?' Jackson grinned, his teeth white in the moonlight. 'It reminds them I'm still here. They'll miss me when I'm gone.'

'Like a hole in the head.'

A clock struck, kept on striking, each note a low boom across the city. It was midnight. Mr Henry would be out and about rat-catching, creeping over rooftops, climbing buildings, sitting on windowsills, peering in at people who should be asleep.

'So apart from drawing,' Jackson said, as if talking about himself was suddenly boring, 'what else do you do?'

'Football,' Megan answered.

Jackson made a pillow of his arms. 'Football? You watch it, right?'

'I play it.'

'But you're a girl! Girls don't do football,' Jackson mocked. 'I don't know what Becky and Laura will say about that! And Kipper, come to think of it. You're meant to do proper girl stuff, like . . . I don't know . . . clothes, shopping, make-up.'

'That's not all girls do!'

'Isn't it? The girls *I* know don't play football.'

Megan rolled her eyes. 'Well . . . duh . . . ! I do!' There was a pause while Jackson digested this.

'Any good?'

'I was the only girl in the school team,' she answered. 'We were doing all right.'

Jackson made a noise, which she supposed meant he was impressed. 'You must be good, then.'

The defiance left her. What was the point of talking about something she might not do again? She'd never be as good and they'd hardly let her back on the team, after so long away from it.

'I *was*.'

'Hey, it'll be OK. You'll see.' Jackson might have been reading her mind. 'When they let us out of here for good, I'm back in the band and you're back in the

84

squad.' He yawned and stretched once more, his limbs looking even longer, more supple, more sinewy. He nudged his drip stand out of the way to make more room. 'In fact, they're letting me out. Tomorrow.'

'Home?' Megan's heart tripped. How would she get through to the end of this week without him? 'For good?'

'Nah. Back in a few weeks.' There was a pause. Megan looked over at him. He was gazing at her. 'Will you be here?'

'Maybe.'

Jackson said nothing, as if he hadn't heard, or didn't care either way. Or perhaps it was because he was no longer awake. He was breathing slowly, rhythmically; there was an occasional little snore. His knees moved slightly, one on top of the other, as he settled further into sleep. There was a twitch of his arm. Megan watched the rise and fall of his chest, watched as the moon came back out and found him, resting its light on his skin.

He had taken off his hat. Long fingers curled around the rim as he held it across his lean stomach. It breathed along with him.

Megan yawned. They should both be back in their own rooms. If the night staff came in, there'd be trouble. Double trouble. But she didn't care, not if Jackson didn't.

Megan curled up into a comfortable ball. She closed her eyes and saw herself and Jackson moving through the city, wrapped in strings of light. They headed further and further away from the hospital till they were just small specks in the black night, walking straight through till dawn.

Seven

Jackson was going home. He was busy packing his stuff with his mum. Megan left them to it though she wanted to be in the room with them. Which was stupid. She'd be going home herself in a couple of days. What a wimp to get upset. She could look after herself. She wasn't a kid. She'd go walkabout on her own.

Only perhaps she'd just have a wander to the main ward, rather than round the whole hospital. She was still tired. It didn't take much to have her wanting to lie back down and sleep. Not that sleeping helped. She still woke up tired.

Megan pushed her drip stand along the corridor in the opposite direction to Jackson's room, nudged through the double doors, and the first thing she saw was Kipper.

Her face was stormy and pink. She was sitting in the middle of her bed. Siobhan was with her. So was her mum, who only barely resembled the woman who'd talked to her the other night. She looked like she'd just got out of bed after a sleepless week.

'Don't want it,' Kipper was saying.

'It's just medicine. To make you feel better,' her mum said. 'Siobhan's brought it special. Just for you.'

Kipper shook her head.

Her mum tried again.

Nothing.

The whole thing was being watched by a small child who was lying on his side clutching a teddy bear which was wearing a tiny nurse's cap with a big red cross on it. His fingers dug deeply into the teddy's tummy, so that it doubled over as if in agony.

'It's just a tiny wee cup,' Siobhan said. 'And it'll make you feel better.'

'No. It won't.'

'Mikey's had his, haven't you, Mikey?' The small boy with the teddy bear nodded. 'See! And he's feeling better, aren't you?'

Another nod. The teddy bear's cap slipped.

Kipper twisted her mouth.

The phone rang at the Nurses' Station. A doctor, shuffling papers about as if looking for one important thing, picked up and listened. 'Sister Brewster, it's for you.' He waved the receiver in the air and continued with his search.

'I'll take it. She's busy.' A nurse appeared behind him, took the phone out of his hand and began to talk into it.

Meanwhile, a baby cried and its mum hushed it with a stroke of its head. A toddler banged the side of his cot with Thomas the Tank Engine, who didn't seem to mind, whose smile stayed put.

A woman with a 'Physiotherapist' badge pinned to her white tunic sat with another child, making him breathe in and out to see if the stuffed mouse on his chest would move. 'There you are. That's much better. Nice deep breaths make the mouse move. You're just like a trampoline!' The boy looked up at her with amazed eyes. 'Clever little man! Let's try some more.'

Then Jackson was there, standing at the top of the ward.

Without his drip and with a jacket and jeans, a small rucksack over his shoulder, he looked normal. No, not normal. He looked stunning.

The whole ward seemed to pause as a number of eyes turned to gaze at him. Even the steady click of machines appeared to stutter for a second as if caught off guard by him.

Megan smiled. He'd come to see her before he'd left. There was a tingle of happiness, an ache of regret. But Jackson headed straight for Kipper, who stopped complaining. The boy with the teddy bear gazed up at him. Thomas the Tank Engine stopped in mid-air.

The mouse moved up and down but the child was peering past the shoulder of the physiotherapist.

'Hiya, Siobhan, what you got there?' Jackson took the small pot of medicine from her hand and waved it under his nose. He closed his eyes as if it was the best thing ever. 'Hmmm,' he said, nodding. 'Essence of strawberry. A hint of ice cream. A scatter of hundreds and thousands.' He opened his eyes once more, made them enormous. There was a giggle from somewhere. 'Can I have this, please?'

Siobhan shook her head. 'Now, Jackson, you know it's not for you. Give it back this minute. You've got your own to take home with you.' Her voice sparkled with amusement.

Jackson frowned at her. '*You're* going to drink it, aren't you? I don't believe it! A nurse! Stealing Kipper's medicine?' He held it up high, out of Siobhan's reach.

Kipper watched open-mouthed, eyes big as barrels. Her mum sat with a faint smile on her lips and pushed back a strand of hair from her face.

'I shall return this to its rightful owner,' said Jackson, tipping the medicine into Kipper's mouth before she could clamp it shut. Very gently he closed her mouth, his fingers resting under her chin, to stop her spitting it back out.

The medicine was gone.

Another giggle from somewhere. Thomas the

Tank Engine clattered into the cot side. The mouse rose and fell. The teddy bear's cap slipped right off.

'See you later, Kipper! And if you have any more trouble with that Siobhan sneaking off with your medicine, you just speak to me or my friend Megan.'

He moved towards Megan and laid his hand gently on her shoulder. It felt warm and nice, like the hand of someone old and wise and kind. For a moment, Megan thought he might want to kiss her again. In front of the whole ward. What would she do? Let him? Megan looked up at him, as if to say, *It's all right, I don't mind if you do.*

But Jackson only smiled at her. 'See you next time, maybe.'

And he was gone.

Megan sat at the Play-Doh table, protecting Kipper's cat. Somehow, and she wasn't entirely sure how, she found herself helping to make a miniature Play-Doh Brian. He was snow-white with blue eyes. They'd only just finished when Kipper had to go back to her bed so that some student doctors could have a look at her. It could take ages, but she made Megan promise to take care of her model.

It was the day before Megan was due to go home and it seemed strange, the idea of losing the drip and stand, her constant companion for what felt like for ever, and to know that she could do ordinary things again.

Ordinary things. What were they?

She looked around at the ward. There was some singing going on. A mum and a nurse with a CD player, singing along with the music. Sitting on a blanket in front of them was a little boy copying them. *Wrinkle your nose*, they sang. The boy wrinkled his nose. *Run your hands through your hair*. He ran his hands over his bald head. *Let your whole self wriggle, wriggle, wriggle*. He flung his arms about, danced his head around and giggled, then clapped because he was so clever.

His skin was a pale yellow and there were small ulcers around his mouth, but that didn't seem to bother him. And when the music stopped with a fanfare and the adults applauded, he just yelled for more.

The play button was pressed again and the song and dance routine resumed.

Bored with waiting for Kipper, and with watching the little boy dance around on his bottom, Megan began to make a nice place for Brian to live. Rolling the dough into sausages for trees, and patting flat green circles for foliage, tiny red balls for apples, she made a garden. It blossomed by the white fence, which overlooked a sky-blue pond with a duck in the middle.

With each piece, Megan concentrated on textures, giving leaves veins, giving trees bark, the pond lilies and the apples sprigs of green, so that everything looked vibrant, alive and splashed with every colour available.

The play specialist nodded approval, while one child slid off her bed, leaving her mother behind, to have a look at the growing garden. One boy dragged his blanket with him, slipped the corner into his mouth and sat sucking it as he watched. The owner of Thomas the Tank Engine shuffled to the end of his cot and peered through the bars. The dancing boy was soon carried over by his mother and this new distraction made him smile all over again.

If Jackson had been there, he might have spun a story around all the models in their startlingly bright colours. In his absence Megan did what she could.

Here was Brian after his sleep.

Here was Brian searching the pond for fish.

Here was Brian climbing one of the trees.

Kipper was on her way back at last, demanding to see her cat, to see if he was safe. Her mum was made to stay by her bed.

Proud of her Play-Doh garden, Megan stood and took Kipper's hand. 'Close your eyes.' Kipper closed her eyes. Megan led her to the table. 'Now open them.'

Kipper blinked into the light, took one look at Brian's new home and her face changed into something quite ugly. She let out a shriek, ran at the garden, and thumping her fist down on to the trees, flattened them one by one.

'No!' she cried with each thump. 'No. No. No.'

It took only seconds to turn Brian's garden, with all of its colour, into a muddy mess.

Six pairs of eyes blinked, gazing curiously at the

mess on the table and the destruction of the garden. Kipper's mum came over, slowly, as if this sort of thing happened all the time.

Nonplussed, Megan rescued the cat but only by a second. 'What's the matter? I thought you'd like it. Doesn't Brian like it?' She waved the cat in front of Kipper's face, which was spotted with angry red blotches.

'No. He hates it.' She swiped the Play-Doh cat out of Megan's hands and threw him to the floor and, with her perfect pink slippers and glittering toes, stamped him flat.

Megan sat with her mouth open and no idea what had gone wrong. Nurses came running. The Play specialist began to clean up the mess.

'Come on, love,' Kipper's mum said. 'Megan's spent all that time making it. Just for you. That's not a nice way to behave.'

'Don't want it. It's stupid.'

'It's all right,' Megan said. 'I was just bored. Just playing. It wasn't very good or anything.'

Kipper stood there staring at the mess and began to cry.

Her mum took her by the hand. 'Come on, love. Time for a rest, I think.'

When she was finally persuaded to go back to her bed, she curled up on it, still crying, as if the whole world, once again, had collapsed around her and was as flat and messy as Brian's garden.

Later, Kipper's mum knocked on Megan's door. 'Just came to say sorry.'

'It doesn't matter. Honestly.'

'Don't know what gets into 'er. One minute she's fine and the next . . . Thinks she can do whatever she likes, that girl. I get so mad with 'er . . .'

Megan smiled. 'It's being in here. It's all the treatment and everything. I wish I could do what she does half the time. And maybe she thought I'd put too many trees in the garden. I mean, Brian could have climbed up any one of them and got lost. And no fire engine to rescue him.'

Kipper's mum shook her head but gave a half-laugh. 'You're a noodle, you are, just like that Jackson. But thanks, anyway. She likes you, just as much as she does 'im. She'll miss you when you go.' A shadow swept across her face then, as if the mention of home was just another thing to worry about. 'Best get back to 'er. Lord knows what she's up to.'

'Will she be going home soon?'

Kipper's mum pressed her lips together and seemed to have to think of an answer. 'They've got a few more things to try. 'Er bloods are all to pot and, well, who knows. See you, love. Tek care of yourself.'

Next morning, Megan sat with her suitcase in the visitors' waiting room while Mum spoke to Sister Brewster. Her bed was stripped bare, the locker

95

emptied, every little indication that Megan had stayed there for almost one hundred and twenty hours had been cleared away, as if a huge vacuum cleaner had come in and sucked it all up.

One hundred and twenty hours.

And it had taken just half an hour to clear it out for the next patient.

Home.

Gemma and the Twins, now that they knew she was on her way, were sending texts like they'd just been invented. They were *dying* to see her, the Twins said. What a funny word to use. In the circumstances. They wanted to know about doctors. Male doctors to be precise. And did she fancy any of them? Which said everything about them.

☺☺☺☺☺☺☺☺☺ came from Gemma, which said everything about her.

'Right, Megan.' Sister Brewster stood at the door. She looked even taller – maybe it was the low seats in the waiting room. 'You've got your return date, so we'll expect you then. Any questions?'

'Will Jackson be here when I get back?' *Please* let him be back next time. If cancer didn't get her, boredom might.

Sister Brewster pondered. 'Off the top of my head, I can't say.' Megan must have shown her disappointment. 'I know this place is not the same when he's not here. It runs more smoothly, that's for sure, but don't worry, you haven't seen the last of him! He's in and out all the time.' She clasped her hands. No more about Jackson. 'So, home! Excited?'

'It'll be great to be in my own bed again.' Megan tried to remember her room at home and couldn't. She might have been away for years, not just days.

She couldn't remember the colour of her walls, or her duvet. Or the curtains or the pictures. It was all locked away somewhere in her head and wouldn't come out.

Maybe that's the effect of having a tumour.

Mind-numbing.

Mum smiled. 'I can't wait to have her home, and we're going to have a houseful!'

Megan looked at her. 'How come?'

'That's a secret.' Mum grinned.

A small commotion outside made them turn to the door. It was Kipper. She was wearing a bright red woollen hat. Her mother was pushing her in a blue wheelchair.

'Is Megan going?'

'Yes, I am.' Megan made her way to the door. Kipper looked very small somehow, her skin so pale it might almost not be there. 'I was just coming to see you, to say bye-bye. Where're you going?'

'She's going to . . .'

'Mam! Megan's *my* friend,' Kipper said, her voice sharp. Her mum looked away, her cheeks flushing. 'I 'ave to go to X-ray.'

So at least they were still friends – she was

forgiven for making the garden and too many trees for Brian to climb. If that's what it was. She was absolved from the crime of trying to cheer up a little girl and failing miserably.

'X-ray? So we all know what that's like . . .' Megan said.

'Boring.'

Sister Brewster smiled. 'Well, Megan has to get home now, Kipper. Off you go!'

The young girl gave a wave and ordered her mum to push her down the corridor.

Eight

There were balloons on the door. Three bright yellow balloons with the words *Welcome*, *Home*, and *Megan*, drawn on them. Mum stood there beaming at her but moved aside with a wink. 'The balloons weren't my idea, by the way.'

'So who . . . ? Dad? Is he back?'

'He's got some leave and he's going to be here in a couple of days, but no. It's not his idea either. You'll just have to wait and see. Let's get everything in. You go ahead. And I want you to lie down on the sofa. You look tired.'

'I'm all right.'

'No arguments. I'll get your bag from the car.'

Megan opened the door and that familiar smell of home hit her. The lavender conditioner Mum used on the clothes, the polish she sprayed the furniture with. Everything sparkling and clean as if a special guest was arriving.

Had she done all of this for her? Because she was home?

Megan looked at the sofa. There was a pillow and a blanket already there. On the coffee table, her *Friends* DVDs. A bag of Liquorice Allsorts. Ready and waiting. As if she'd run away from home but had come back and everything had to be perfect, in case she ran away again.

Oh, Mum.

And she was puzzled. Where was everybody? There wasn't a houseful at all. What had she been going on about before?

'I'm just making a drink,' Mum called through. 'Want a cup of tea? Or cocoa?'

'No thanks.'

'Juice?'

'I'm fine, Mum.'

Megan stood in the middle of the lounge and listened to the house and all of its noises. She could hear children playing in the street, their shrieks and cries, their tussles with each other. She could hear a football being kicked about. She made her way to the window and looked out. The three kids from next door were playing with the two from Number 5. They pounded up and down the pavement until, shouting a warning, they scattered like flies. The Bakers' car was coming, turning into Number 19.

She had just begun to babysit for the Bakers when her dizziness stopped her. Their daughter was two and a half and called her Melon, and whenever she did, Megan could only think of those big green and red ones with all the pips. The ones she hated.

The Bakers had sent her a card from their daughter. It had lots of scrunched-up paper stuck on the front and a wild scribble of crayon inside. She'd stuck it to the wall behind her bed along with all the other cards. She had used Blu-Tack and when her cards came down, that last day, there were little blue remnants all over the place. She wasn't sure what the cleaning staff would think of that.

Megan counted the children outside. Ten of them now. She found herself wondering how many would end up in hospital with cancer, or if she was going to be the only one round here.

Eeeny. She put her finger on the glass and pointed at the curly blond boy. Meeny. The red-haired girl. Miny. The dark-haired one with long pigtails. Mo . . . The car from Number 7 backed out of its drive. There was a warning cry and the children scattered like leaves. Mo . . . thought Megan. Me.

It was Gemma who pushed open the door. It was Gemma who grinned and threw herself at Megan. 'Hiya!' she said, as if they'd never been apart, as if she hadn't *not* visited her in hospital. As if there hadn't been one hundred and twenty hours of no friends.

The Twins hung back slightly, like two uncertain deer.

So this was the *houseful*.

'Hi, Megan. How're you feeling?' That was Frieda.

'Good? Or bad? Do you feel bad? You look all right.' That was Stacey.

They were both frowning behind their fringes, as if saying just those few words was too hard, as if they weren't used to talking.

The Twins?

Not used to talking?

'I'm OK,' Megan replied. 'Are you not coming in?'

The girls shuffled into the room. They were so identical that even their movements and emotions seemed synchronised. Today they appeared to be terrified and stared at Megan as if she were an unexploded bomb or had the plague.

Gemma touched her arm in that quiet way of hers. 'Was it horrible?'

'No, not really . . . it was . . .'

'We're sorry we didn't visit or anything but, anyway . . . We brought the balloons. Do you like them?' Stacey looked as if the balloons were a bad idea.

Megan tried to answer.

'When're you coming back to school?' Frieda sprang into action. 'You've missed *so* much work.

Did they make you do any? Are you in tomorrow?' She flopped into a chair.

There was silence for a second. Megan wished it would go on for longer. She wished they'd all just go home.

'She's not going to be in *tomorrow*, stupid, she's just got out of hospital!' Stacey flopped into another chair.

'Yes, but it's *PE*.' Frieda shook her head as if all sisters were stupid. 'And we know what Megan's like when it comes to that! Football . . .'

They sat looking expectantly at her. Gemma said nothing, just played with her earring, rolling it around in her ear lobe.

'I don't think I can do it. I've still got a drip thing in,' Megan said.

The Twins blinked. 'Where?'

Megan patted her collarbone. 'It's in here. I have to keep it in till the treatment's finished. I can't get it wet.'

'Ugh!' There was an exchange of looks between the Twins. 'But . . . it's not finished?' Frieda said.

'Have they not got rid of it?' That was Stacey.

Gemma tutted. 'She's just on her first treatment. They told us at school, remember!'

'Did they?' Megan said. Then she remembered Mum telling her she'd gone to see the Head. But the thought of going back with everyone knowing . . .

'Mrs Delaney's had cancer and she said she had to

103

have lots of treatments. So you might, as well. That's what she told us.' Gemma glanced at Megan. 'Just to us, you know. To our class.'

'Her hair fell out,' Frieda said, sliding a look at Megan.

'But you'd never know,' said Stacey. 'I've never noticed. Mrs Delaney's hair's always looked rubbish.' A sideways glance at Megan.

Even Gemma seemed curious.

'It's still all mine,' she said, giving it a tug.

The Twins breathed a sigh of relief. 'Good,' they said. Up they got. 'But we have to go now. Mum said we weren't to stay long . . .' They made a fuss of finding the present they'd brought. A box of chocolates. 'Just in case we made you worse.'

Megan had to smile.

'So when will you be back?' the Twins said.

'Don't know. Maybe next week. I've got the work they sent me.'

'If you need any more, I can bring it,' Gemma offered. 'Any time.'

The Twins were at the door. 'You didn't tell us about the doctors? Any nice ones?'

Megan pictured the staff. Her drawings of them. The frog consultant, the long lanky doctor with spiky hair who looked like a sweeping brush.

'Yeah. Loads,' she said, 'if you get bored gnawing your arm off.'

There was a delicious moment of quiet after the

front door closed – with a bang – behind the Twins. The whole house seemed to take a breath and sigh, then the normal sounds drifted back in. Mum in the kitchen. The clock on the mantelpiece.

Megan curled up on the sofa with Gemma and watched a couple of episodes of *Friends*. They laughed at the bits they always laughed at and yet it didn't feel all that funny. Not any more. They had such stupid things go wrong with them. They were like a walking problem page. None of it real.

'Are you tired?' Gemma asked. 'I can stay. Or go.'

Megan flicked off the TV. 'I don't know. I feel like I've been hit by something very big and very fast.'

Gemma giggled. 'That would be the Twins.'

Megan smiled, but she was tired. She closed her eyes and thought about what to do for the rest of the day, the rest of the week and all the weeks till she went back into hospital and saw Jackson again.

It was all mixed up. She never wanted to go back and yet where else would she see him? It was like watching a big black cloud inching nearer and nearer, but wanting it to come, wanting it to rain right on top of you, because you'd feel rain, you'd feel it on your skin and on your hair and it would be real.

'I don't think I can come back to school. Not yet. It'll be like a class *full* of Twins.'

Gemma was frowning. 'Are you all right? Will I get your mum?'

Not Mum. What she wanted right then was Jackson. 'I'm fine. But I think I need to go to sleep. Is that OK?'

'Course it is. I'll go now. Ring you later?' Gemma gave her a tight hug. It felt too tight, as if she were trying too hard.

'I'll ring you,' Megan said. 'I might sleep right through till tomorrow, I'm so whacked.'

Or maybe till she could go back. Till she could see Jackson again.

Nine

But it wasn't until her third treatment that she saw Jackson again and when she discovered him on the ward, in his old room, as if he'd never left it, Megan had to stop herself from smiling. This was right. This feeling. Just seeing him again.

The last time she was in hospital hadn't felt right at all, him not being there. Going home afterwards hadn't either, or getting back to school, where she'd had to listen to the Twins going on about stupid stuff like clothes and getting their belly buttons pierced and that new maths teacher who was *just gorgeous*. And Gemma joining in as if that's all she thought about too. It was rubbish. Everything.

At least she was here now, trying to persuade Jackson to let her draw him.

'I've done almost everyone else. Do you want to see them?'

He didn't show any interest. He just lay back on his bed, eyes closed. And he didn't seem all that pleased to see her.

For the first time Megan wondered if he had a girlfriend, someone he'd seen when he was at home, someone lovely and healthy and not with cancer. Someone who didn't remind him of what he had.

Maybe cancer made you imagine that people liked you more than they really did. Megan tried not to think about that.

'Well, can I draw you?'

'Do I have to move?'

Megan giggled. 'No.'

'OK, then.'

Grandad had been asking about her drawings. He said while she couldn't play football she should draw as much as possible. She could be a proper artist, if only she'd practise. And he wanted to see some of her pictures – she would have to send him a few. She could send him this one, of Jackson.

'Ah, you're here.' Sister Brewster peered in. 'Nice to see you back, Megan. What're you up to?' She gave them both a smile.

Megan gestured at her sketch pad. 'Jackson's a rubbish model.'

Sister Brewster didn't seem surprised at that.

'I'm glad I've got you both together, because, Jackson, if you're planning any walkabouts this time . . .'

'Yeah,' Jackson said, not opening his eyes. 'What?'

'It would be really useful if you could just give us a hint. I know we've had it far too easy, these last few weeks, with you being at home, but easy is how we prefer it. And you could take Megan with you. Maybe she'll keep you out of trouble.'

There was a pause. A meaningful look.

Megan frowned. Why was Sister Brewster going on like this?

'So, what d'you say? Is that a plan?'

Jackson didn't respond. Either he didn't want Sister Brewster on his case, or he didn't want anyone to go with him on his travels, as if it might delay him, or make it more difficult.

For a moment, Megan thought he was going to refuse. She gave him a prod.

'OK,' Jackson said, with a roll of his eyes. He didn't bother with his usual grin, always at the ready to smooth things over. 'So we'll go later, to . . . the old part. Megan hasn't seen it.'

'That's fine, but don't be too long. Remember, we haven't got the time or the staff to come hunting for you . . .' Off she went.

'Bog off, Rooster,' he muttered.

Megan felt like she'd been dropped into another conversation entirely. 'What's wrong?'

Jackson shook his head but said nothing, just stared at the ceiling.

'She's only making a point, that's all,' Megan went on.

Still no response.

'Has something happened?'

'Nothing. Nothing's *happened*.'

Silence.

Megan ran her fingers along the side of her sketch pad. There were lots of pages in it. The whole thing felt solid, reliable, something you could trust to do what you expected it to do. Like trees. Rocks.

What was wrong with Jackson?

'Last time I was in,' she said, aware that she was almost gabbling, 'there was no one. Nobody to talk to. Siobhan was away on holiday. And they've got some new nurses. New patients. Everything. I would have talked to Becky and Laura but they weren't even about because Becky's brother went home, and so did Kipper. But she's back in. I think.'

Jackson seemed not to be listening but he turned his eyes to her. 'So did you get back to school at all?'

'A bit,' she replied. 'After my second treatment. Do you get used to chemo? I didn't feel so tired last time.' There was no reply. 'Anyway, I was only in half-days.'

She'd hated it. Every second of it. Mum dropped her off on her first day back and she'd almost panicked. Just froze in her seat.

It didn't get any better.

'I've got this friend, Gemma,' Megan went on. 'She was great, but we aren't in the same lessons all the time and then there's Stacey and Frieda.' She shook her head. 'They're really nice, but treat you like you're . . . I don't know what . . . like something from a zoo. And everyone else. They keep waiting for my hair to fall out or something, or to turn green.'

Jackson nodded as if he knew all about that.

'I was glad to be back. It sounds stupid, but I was.' Back on the ward where it didn't matter what you looked like, or if you felt rotten. Everyone was the same. 'Did you go to school?'

'In and out,' Jackson said. 'I'm always just in and out of school. They're used to it. And I hardly do any work. They don't make me. Cancer has its good points.'

Megan looked for one of his grins. It didn't come. Something deep inside her gave a flutter. What was wrong with him? Why was he in such a mood?

'Someone asked me if I was pregnant,' she said, hoping to raise a smile, cos I've been away so much.'

More silence. Megan gazed across at Jackson. He was bored, obviously, didn't want her here. He didn't want her with him, anywhere.

She gathered up her things and stood to go, trying

111

not to remember that once he'd kissed her as if he liked her, trying not to feel hurt.

'Will you come and get me?' she said. 'Later? If you're feeling all right?'

Megan waited at the door. What would she do if he said no?

At last Jackson looked up. 'Yeah. I will.'

The old part of the hospital seemed to be nothing but corridors covered in green tiles. It was a maze. Along the walls were tall windows, with sills you could sit on they were so deep, and glass divided up into small panes which looked out over red-brick buildings of all shapes and sizes. A dull afternoon light struggled in.

Megan and Jackson walked past dark passage-ways on each side, with arched entrances, like tunnels. The corridor dipped slowly towards its destination. There were signs for Rheumatology, Endocrinology, Pathology, Haematology.

Jackson was quiet. He'd come to get Megan from her room, as promised, said he was going for a walk and waited for her. She forgave his mood and was pleased, but none of it was fun. He really didn't want her company, he was doing it because Sister Brewster had told him to. It was obvious.

'Where are we going exactly?' Megan asked.

'Dunno,' Jackson said. 'Never got to the end of this corridor yet.'

They'd been walking for some time, pushing their drip stands along in front of them.

A doctor strode by, with a stethoscope wrapped around his neck. He seemed to be in a world of his own. Five minutes later, a woman with a stick struggled towards them, appearing out of nowhere, it seemed. She was dumpy, with whiskers, a nest of white hair and complete bewilderment on her face.

'Have you seen the Eye Department, pet?' she wheezed. 'Must have come the wrong way.' Megan glanced at Jackson who shook his head and shrugged. 'It's the opfimology I want,' the woman continued. She pushed an appointment card at them.

'Oph-thal-mology,' Megan read.

'That's it, pet. Opfimology.'

'It says it's in Spencer Wing . . . where's that, Jackson?'

He was beginning to move away, as if nothing mattered except a corridor he'd never reached the end of.

A smartly dressed woman came by, hair plaited into a thick, silver rope. There was an official badge pinned to her jacket. She knew exactly where Spencer Wing was.

'It's for this lady,' explained Megan. 'We know where we're going.'

'But the children's ward's at the other end of the hospital, isn't it?' This was more of a statement than a question and suggested that this woman, with her name badge, thought they were up to something. 'What are you doing all the way down here?' The woman looked hard at Jackson. 'Aren't you the boy who . . .'

Megan frowned. The boy who what?

The lady in search of Ophthalmology gave another confused smile. '*You'll* show me where I need to be,' she pleaded. 'I'm going to be ever so late.'

There was a moment, a flash of something in the woman's face, as if she had a lot more to say. But now wasn't the time. She turned her gaze to the old lady. 'Of course I will, dear.'

Off they went, but not before Megan and Jackson were given another very doubtful look from the woman with the silver plait.

'What a nose *she* is,' Megan said when they'd gone, 'with her briefcase and everything. Probably a secretary or something.'

'Or a floor cleaner.'

Megan looked at Jackson. He was smiling at last. Grinning even.

'Toilet scrubber,' she said.

As they wandered along the corridor once more, they whittled down the woman's rank to less than a cockroach and left it at that.

It was tiring, this aimless walking. Megan noticed silver beads of moisture on Jackson's skin and was moving more slowly.

'Are you OK?'

'New treatment,' he said, as if this answered everything.

Megan was grateful to see two chairs outside the laundry department. 'We've come too far.' It began to worry her, the journey back. The thought of being safe on the ward was so inviting that she wished they could hitch a ride on one of those whining little cars the porters drove.

'What was that woman going on about?'

'Who?'

'The woman with the plait. Weren't you the boy . . . who did what? Have you been in more trouble?' Jackson shook his head, his face suddenly stony. 'OK, OK. I don't want to know. None of my business.'

Later, still sitting there, Jackson had moved from one mood to another, in the way only he could. The butterfly. He was cheerful at last, telling Megan all about his great-grandfather's trumpet playing. He stopped mid-sentence and slipped the *famous* hat off his head to examine it.

'What's wrong?' Megan asked.

'Nothing. But isn't this a cool hat?' It was old, it was a bit of a mess, certainly not cool. 'It's like, I wear this and he's here, see? Like his music's still here.'

'In the hat?' Megan whipped it out of his fingers to have a look inside, checking for music.

Jackson whisked it back. 'Like he's never really gone. Like he's here still.'

'Sort of a ghost, you mean?'

There was a pause. 'Yeah, sort of.'

Megan waved her fingers in front of him. '*Whoooooooh*. Tell us a spooky story, Jackson,' she mimicked a nine-year-old.

He gave her a look as if she were behaving just like one. 'So, how old did you say your grandad was?'

Jackson moving again. From flower to flower. Never staying still. 'Isn't he a hundred or something?'

'Almost,' Megan answered. 'He's ninety-six next birthday.'

'Wow! That's just *so* ancient! My great-grandad might have been a hundred now if he hadn't died.'

It had never really occurred to Megan that Grandad was particularly ancient; old, yes, older than anyone else's grandfather, but so what? He was just Grandad.

'I can't work this out,' Jackson was saying. 'He's nearly a hundred years old and you're, what, fifteen?'

'Fourteen. Almost fourteen,' Megan said, pleased he'd thought her older. He looked up at the ceiling, nodding as if counting or singing to himself. He did a lot of that, as if he had music permanently playing inside his head. 'And your mum's how old?'

Megan did a sum in her head. 'Forty-seven, nearly. She says Grandad married late.'

'Class!'

'What? Marrying late?'

Jackson was looking at her seriously. 'You wouldn't lie, right?' Megan shook her head wondering what he was thinking, where this was leading. 'So he was still at it when he was pushing *fifty*.'

Megan thought for a second or two. Then it dawned on her. 'Jackson!'

He grinned and punched the air. 'That's some going!'

'Don't! Leave him alone!' Megan buried her face in her hands, hair folding down around them. 'That's my grandad you're talking about!' Then she was laughing, despite everything. It was terrible, this talk about him doing THAT, but she couldn't stop. Her sides ached, her face burned, her eyes streamed, but it was so good to have the old Jackson back.

At last Megan was able to look at him without giggling. He was gazing at her, eyes half closed, with a smile on his face, as if he knew all about stuff like that, as if he was thinking about it right now.

She pushed a hand through her hair, taking it clumsily back off her cheek. Maybe he was going to put his arm around her again, here in the middle of the corridor with people appearing out of nowhere. She met his gaze. She wouldn't mind at all, even if the whole hospital turned up. If he wanted to. She wouldn't stop him.

He was still smiling, as if he'd always known this.

Megan frowned, her heart giving a tiny stutter. Something felt odd. She gazed at her hand for a long moment, hardly knowing what had happened. A tangle of hair was wrapped around her fingers, the sort of tangle you get when you clean a hairbrush.

For a second she wondered who it belonged to, wondered how it got there.

Then she knew.

'Jackson?' she whispered, trembling. She held up her hand, and watched the smile die on his lips.

'Right!' Jackson said. 'Back to the ward.' He pulled her from the chair, his hand strong around hers.

Megan stared down at the pure black fingers wrapped around hers. Her hand looked pale and tiny in his. It felt weak. It didn't belong to her. It was his now, not hers. Nothing belonged any more.

Everything about her was sucked out and she was wobbly with it, from her knees to her stomach, to her heart. Even her breath came out in little pieces.

'It'll be all right,' Jackson said, his voice quiet, assured. A squeeze of her hand. 'It's what happens with chemo.'

A group of young doctors appeared, laughing like a flock of gulls. They all seemed to have heads full of hair, all colours, thick, glossy. The sort you could run your fingers through and not have it fall out. Safe. Real. Healthy.

Not a bald one among them.

Their shirts looked brand new, as if they'd just bought them, and were neatly tucked in, nothing flapping or untidy. Curved round their necks were shining stethoscopes; their pockets bulged with notebooks.

Everything about them was fresh and gleaming. Unused. Like new cars in showrooms, the sort everybody wants to buy.

Megan felt full of dents and scratches. A car nobody would want to buy. How dare they laugh when her hair was falling out? Couldn't they see she had cancer? Couldn't they see what was happening? What kind of doctors were they, not noticing things?

'Students,' Jackson declared, his eyes following them as they swooped round the bend in the corridor, disappearing out of view. 'They go round in packs.'

'Let's go,' Megan said, still clinging on to Jackson's hand. She wanted to be back in the safety of the ward, the comfort of her own room. She wanted to hide under the bedclothes and never come out again. 'Please, Jackson. Let's go now.'

Somehow she managed not to cry on the way. Somehow, she managed to put one foot in front of the other and not think about anything. Somehow she managed to take breaths in and take breaths out. Worse than exams. Worse than the dentist's.

They got back to the ward without saying anything much at all.

Megan was almost pleased to see the elephant's pink toenails, almost happy to hear a baby scream and a telephone ring.

And there was Siobhan.

'So, you two . . .' the nurse paused, glancing at their joined hands.

Megan tried to slide her fingers free from Jackson's, but he just gripped more tightly. She looked up at his face and saw defiance there, in the set of his mouth, and the way he looked down at Siobhan.

'Back at last, hey? I think Sister was expecting you a *wee* bit earlier than this . . .' Jackson was about to speak, but Siobhan stopped him. 'Don't tell me where you've been. I'll only have to report it. And next time . . . don't be away so long.' A pause when they all seemed to look at each other and not know what to say. At last Siobhan smiled at them. 'Never mind. We're having the changeover. See you later.'

Megan had to go, had to think about what was happening to her hair, had to cry. Desperately. She trailed her hand from Jackson's. The emptiness felt like pain in her fingers.

'I want to go to sleep,' she said.

Jackson glanced up and down the corridor and seemed satisfied. 'Don't, not yet. I'll fix it.'

'I don't know what you mean.'

'Don't worry.' Jackson put his arm around her shoulders, headed for her door and pushed her gently through it.

Gazing around her room, everything was so familiar, everything in its right place. The locker by her bed, the cupboard on the wall behind, the call button. The door to the shower and toilet, slightly ajar, the way she'd left it. The curtains still hanging from the rail, flapping ever so slightly, nudged by the breeze from outside.

Nothing had changed since she left to go with Jackson.

So why her? Not everyone's hair fell out. She'd read it somewhere. Hadn't she? So why couldn't she be one of the ones it didn't happen to?

She didn't want to lose her hair, but the proof was still there grasped between her fingers. It was coming out.

Perhaps she shouldn't have gone anywhere, perhaps if she'd not wandered down old corridors it wouldn't have happened. Yet Sister Brewster had said to go, to keep Jackson out of trouble, so how did that work?

Before long, he was back. 'So . . . everyone's busy . . .' he said. 'Let's shave it off!' He waved a razor in the air, the sort Dad used on his face. With all the blades.

'My hair?'

Jackson nodded as if to an idiot and waited. He was in no rush, it seemed.

'Mum'll go mad,' Megan said, struck by the awful inevitability of it all. 'And, anyway,' she added, looking at the razor suspiciously, 'where'd you get that?'

'Never mind! Your head's going to start looking like an old mat. So we'll sort it before that happens. Your mum'll be pleased, you'll see. What's it to be? The cool, bare look, or mouldy mat?' Then he stopped. 'Scissors. Oh, and you need to be on one of those chairs.'

Out he went again.

Megan sat on one of the two visitor's chairs. The sun slanted in through the window. It felt warm on her skin but it couldn't shift the chill which had begun to seep into her bones.

She wanted Mum and Dad, she wanted Grandad, she wanted Gemma and Stacey and Frieda, she wanted anyone who could possibly stop this happening, take her away and hide her. But they were all in another bubble somewhere, floating in another sky, and there was no way to reach them.

'Ready?' Jackson was back again with scissors.

'Not really,' she said. 'Just do it.' What did it matter? What did anything matter?

'You'll look great,' Jackson said, pulling another chair over. He sat behind her, his long legs like armrests at either side of her. 'Really, you will.'

She shook her head. She'd look terrible.

'Let's have a look at you.' He ran his fingers

through her hair, like a hairdresser, assessing. 'You could sell this lot, you know.'

'Yeah. Right.' Who'd want the hair of someone with cancer?

She felt dirty. Contaminated. It made her hunch up her shoulders in a kind of shame.

'Hey, come on.' Jackson's fingers moved over her scalp. They felt cool. Relaxing. He was massaging her skin with slow gentle circles, round her ears, up and over the curves and bumps of her skull, over the place where her tumour was supposed to be, up towards her temples, weaving something like sleep into her. A delicious dizziness swept through her and she felt herself almost tipping over. She clamped her hands on to his thighs, which tightened around her as if Jackson knew she was going to fall, enclosing her, breathing her in, so that there was nothing left of her, as if he was saving her from harm.

Megan closed her eyes, resting her head against his hands, allowing it to be pulled towards him. She let it lie against his chest, and felt him under her skin, all the bones of him, his breastbone, the knots of his ribs, and his heart, beating strongly beneath it all, while hers felt quite dead.

Then she let out a great sob, something which rose right from inside her, like a scream suppressed.

'Do it, Jackson.'

'It's OK,' he said. 'Ssssh.'

And he began to cut.

As the first bits of hair fell into her lap Megan picked them up, allowing herself to examine them properly. How soft they were, baby soft almost, and so much colour. She thought her hair was brown, just plain ordinary brown, yet each strand looked different somehow now that it was parted from her head, now that it was lying in the palm of her hand. It was as if each one had taken up a new colour, red or gold, as well as brown.

And she was just noticing it now.

More hair fell in clumps, amputated from her head, bits of it drifting to the floor. Jackson was singing as he snip, snip, snipped away.

No more fussing with her hair. No more bobbles. Or scrunchies. No more shampoo or conditioner. No frizz, no straighteners.

She steadied herself again, clutching at his legs.

Another handful was tugged away from her head, the blades of the scissors chomping around it, as if the work was too hard for them, her hair too thick.

Megan's throat began to ache and wouldn't swallow. Her eyes blurred, so that all around her faded into a watery haze. Nothing felt real any more.

Scissor blades opened and closed, opened and closed, unstoppable as they crunched through her hair. What would they say, when they saw her? Mum, Dad, Grandad, her friends. They'd look and see . . . not her. She wasn't Megan any more.

Jackson, as if only aware of the task he had to

perform, took another handful of hair and chopped through it. Megan watched as everything about her, everything that said who she was, slid down her shoulders and cascaded to the floor, like leaves shaken from a dying tree.

Ten

'What do you think you're doing?' Sister Brewster appeared at the door. There had only been one sweep with the razor so far but it hadn't been at all pleasant. Megan half wondered if Jackson really knew what he was doing. 'Give that to me right now!'

The game was up.

'I was making her look presentable,' Jackson declared, smiling his most winning smile. Sister Brewster wasn't to be won over. She held out her hand, waiting for the razor. 'It's a safety one, can't do any harm.' Jackson, sounding sulky, handed it over, smile all gone.

Sister Brewster shook her head. 'And Megan, I would have thought you had more sense than to let Jackson anywhere near you with this!'

She brandished the razor at them both, her face furious, ranting on about safety regulations, about the dangers of sharp blades. There were babies and toddlers on the ward for goodness' sake, what would have happened if . . . and where on earth was their common sense?

Megan stared at her hands, saying nothing, heart thumping. She closed her eyes in disbelief when Jackson spoke up, his voice sullen, stubborn.

'She lets the doctors at her. What's sensible about that?'

'I beg your pardon?' Sister Brewster faced him.

'Don't, Jackson. It's all right.'

Jackson swung round to face Megan, his face stormy. 'No, it's not all right! You let *them*, why not me? At least *I* was doing some good.'

Megan groaned. She knew when they'd lost, knew there was no point in prolonging the agony.

'Jackson . . .' Sister Brewster stood with her big eyes resting on him, her mouth in a straight line. He should have seen the warning in her face.

'You've never had your hair fall out, have you? You've never had needles stuck in you. Not the way we have. And what good does it do, anyway?'

Something in Jackson's voice made Megan look up. His face was set like stone, though the nerves in his cheeks twitched with anger.

Sister Brewster remained calm. 'It's all very

important, as you well know. We don't stick needles into people for nothing. We don't do it for fun.'

'But what good does it do? You tell me!' He was glaring at Sister Brewster, looking at her as if he hated what he saw.

What was he doing?

Why wouldn't he stop?

'It can do a lot of good, Jackson.' Sister Brewster's voice changed slightly, there was a hint of kindness in it. 'It can. You know that.'

'Like it's helping Kipper?' He spat out the girl's name.

'Let's not discuss her now, Jackson.'

'Why not? You didn't mind *discussing* her when I took her for a walk . . . and you sent the whole army to find us.'

Megan swallowed. What was he on about? What did he mean about Kipper?

'I think it's time you went to your own room, Jackson. You're all finished here.' Sister Brewster straightened her back, which made her even taller than before, and held the door wide open.

It was Siobhan who tidied her up, Siobhan with her long black hair piled high on her head, tiny corkscrew curls framing her face. She had milk-white skin, green eyes.

That lovely Shee-vorn, Grandad once said, *sounds like an angel.*

Megan had seen her once, coming on to the ward. She wasn't on duty, and was wearing ordinary clothes, but her hair tumbled loosely down her back, like a princess in a book. She was wearing a big diamond engagement ring. Somehow Megan hadn't expected that. Siobhan belonged with them on the ward. That she could have another life outside seemed strange.

'You two!' Siobhan said now, cleaning up the last of her hair. 'The Terrible Twins, that's what you are. You mustn't try any more tricks like this. Sister Brewster's scalding mad.'

'He was only trying to help,' Megan said, her voice trembling.

Siobhan turned to face her, hands on hips. 'Next time he tries to help, push that bell and I'll deal with him myself.'

The hair was swept up and tidied away into a paper bag.

Siobhan was looking at her severely but even so, there was a kindness in her face, a softness in her voice. 'You know what?' she said. Megan shook her head. All she knew was that she'd been stupid and so had Jackson. 'I have something that you might like. Shall I go and get it?'

Everything was so strange – her hair in a bag like that, a bag for hospital waste, ready to go into the bin. The air seemed so much colder, her head lighter, as if it didn't belong to her.

'Yes, please,' Megan said, feeling smaller than before, younger, more stupid.

'Now, don't go looking at yourself till I get back. Promise?' Siobhan was at the door. 'You're not bald, exactly, but you're not tidy either. But it's the best we can do for now.'

The word *bald* came as a complete and utter shock to Megan, but that's what Jackson had been aiming at, wasn't it? She desperately wanted to cry, but whisked at her eyes, stopping the tears. 'OK.'

Siobhan was back in no time with a bright red baseball cap. 'Try this on. It's adjustable.' Megan pushed the cap on her head, immediately feeling better. 'But when you go home, get yourself to a hairdresser. Someone who'll do it properly.' She paused. 'Want me to stay while you look in the mirror? It'll be a shock with all that hair gone.'

Her voice was so gentle that Megan did long for her to stay, longed to be wrapped up and held until this nightmare – because suddenly it was a nightmare – ended. And yet this was something she had to do on her own. It was her fault. She'd told Jackson he could do it. Megan shook her head.

'Well, you know where I am.'

'Yes,' Megan said. 'Thank you.'

Siobhan left her with another smile.

Picking up the bag, Megan opened it, staring at the mess nestling in the bottom. She pushed her fingers inside, let the hair sift through them, drift over them like small threads of silk, then she closed the bag, took it over to the bin by the sink and dropped it in. The lid came down with a heavy clunk, like a prison door closing.

It was Kipper who told her the story. It was Kipper who made her mum push her to Megan's room and go away. It was Kipper who demanded to have a feel of Megan's head, her large eyes seeming even bigger, more determined somehow that she wouldn't be refused anything.

'Was Sister Brewster mad at Jackson?' she asked, trailing her fingers through the tufts of Megan's hair. They felt light, papery, her fingers. They tickled.

'At both of us. And when I go home, Mum'll probably be mad as well.' Megan rolled her eyes, as if it didn't really matter. It was only hair.

'Jackson's always getting into trouble. He's very naughty,' Kipper said with a hint of pride in her voice. She smoothed her hand over Megan's head. 'Are you going to get bald and buy a wig? I've got a pink one, but it's itchy.'

Megan supposed she would just have it all shaved off, it was such a mess. Go straight to Mum's hairdresser and get it sorted. 'I'll have to see.'

Kipper sat back with a sigh as if all of a sudden touching her head was boring, or that not knowing which kind of wig to get was a sign of failure.

Megan replaced the red cap, felt its warmth hug her. She glanced at Kipper. It was strange to see her in a wheelchair, a proper one, not the sort you went down to X-ray in.

'Do you want to go back to your bed?'

Kipper shrugged. 'Only Mam, or a nurse, is allowed to push me.'

'Uh-oh. Is that because of Jackson? Do I feel a story coming on?'

There was a big smile in reply and the tale began, Kipper grinning as she told it, her face almost glittering with the fun of it all.

Jackson had been telling some of the children about Mr Henry and they wanted to see him. So he said they could hunt for him on the ward and those who could followed him.

'How many was that?'

Kipper looked puzzled and had to think hard. 'Three. It was three. And they looked behind all the beds and in the bathrooms,' she said, 'but he wasn't there. And they looked in the pillowcase cupboard and he wasn't there either. And Jackson was in the lead . . .'

'Sounds like the Pied Piper,' Megan said, imagining it all. 'The story with rats in it,' she explained when Kipper gave her a baffled look. 'Did you go?'

133

'I just watched. My legs stopped working and I fell down and I hurt all over and Jackson said he'd take me properly. Not just round the beds with the little ones. Round the hospital.'

She was still full of it. Being off the ward with Jackson, being away from all the machines and the babies crying and being sick into dishes, and all the doctors and the dinners that smelled of sweaty socks and tasted of cardboard, and all the people saying hello and smiling at her and saying how good she was and not meaning it because she was always naughty.

'Where was your mum?'

No wonder there was trouble.

'The hairdresser's. We went all the way down the corridor to the front door where the porter men live and we saw the amblinces coming in and making the noise and flashing and everything and we went outside and looked at the grass and saw the birds. Then someone found us and made us go back in.'

'Did you see Mr Henry?'

Kipper shook her head. 'He was asleep.'

Of course, he would be, Megan thought. A ghost cat awake during the day, a ghost cat who might only exist in Jackson's stories.

'So you had a nice time?'

'Yes.' Kipper smiled a huge smile, which faded as she remembered the rest. 'Sister Brewster went mad again. Everyone was looking for us.'

'Bet they were.' Megan frowned, noticing how much paler Kipper was, as if all that talking had sucked the energy out of her, making her slump even further into her chair.

A flicker of alarm. Megan's heart began to thump. She could feel it in her ears. 'Are you tired? Will I get Siobhan? Kipper? Do you need to go back now?' She reached for the bell push.

'I'll take her.' It was Jackson.

Megan shook her head. 'You can't. You're in enough trouble. I'll get a nurse.'

'I said, I'll take her.'

Kipper's eyes flickered towards Jackson for a fleeting second but there was something urgent in her voice. 'I want to see Brian. Will you tell them I want to see him?'

'I'll tell them,' Jackson said.

'Will you say now? I want to go now?'

But how could Kipper go home? Didn't she have more treatment to get? Something new they wanted to try? Hadn't her mum said that? Her bloods were all to pot, she'd said. Maybe they were better now. But if not, how could she see Brian? He was at home. She was here.

Didn't Jackson understand anything?

Couldn't he see that he was just going to make even more trouble?

And yet.

Kipper was smiling now, at the thought of seeing

her kitten. Megan could picture her so easily, away from here, in her own house, on a sofa perhaps, cuddling Brian. She'd be kissing his tiny nose and he'd be purring and digging his claws in just a little to tell her he was happy she was home, and he wouldn't climb any more trees and have to be rescued because Kipper was there holding him. And there'd be no more clicking machines, no more beeps, no more nurses, or drips and needles, just her mum and dad and her pet.

Something about that picture was so perfect, so right, that it made Megan turn away and not try to stop Jackson.

'See you later, Kipper,' she said, as they left.

Could you have enough of treatments? Could you be so fed up with being in hospital that no matter what, you just want to go home? Could you know, when you're not even seven years old yet, that it's not working? All the treatment. Was this the reason for Kipper's bad temper? One minute lovely, the next screaming her head off? So bossy with her mum?

There was a little girl, who had a little curl, right in the middle of her forehead.
When she was good she was very, very good and when she was bad she was horrid.

Megan gazed through the window and saw a lone bird drifting across the clouds which hung in fuzzy white drapes, as if billowed by the wind and frozen into shape. The bird was a gull, she decided, watching it being slowly swallowed by the sky, white into white, until there was nothing left.

Eleven

Megan was back in hospital for her operation and though it meant the end of her treatment, perhaps, she dreaded having her head cut open. What would happen if they found something worse inside?

Deciding not to think of that, she tore the wrapping off one of the new magazines Gemma and the Twins had given her and went straight to the problem page at the back, same as always, and same as always she decided they weren't real. They must pay people to make them up.

Does my boyfriend fancy my best mate?
My mum's got a new partner and he hates me.
I think I'm pregnant.
Same old stuff every time.

They didn't know what problems were. They

should come to this ward and see the real stuff. *They're going to slice my head open – what can I do?*

'Is that glued on? Or does it come off?' Jackson was in her doorway. 'Can I come in?' He stood there as if he'd never walked into her room without asking. 'Pleased to see me?'

Megan grinned. 'No. Yes. Yes. And definitely.'

And it was true, but . . . she took in how his legs looked thinner, each bone sharper than before, like blades pressing through. His eyes were dark caves under the shadow cast by his hat. His skin looked dull. Maybe they were trying another new treatment on him.

She wondered what it was like to be so rare that they couldn't work you out, and to have all sorts of treatments, and things written about you. Wouldn't you just get sick of it? Wouldn't you just want to go away somewhere and never come back?

Shaking these thoughts out of her head she smiled at him. 'You're allowed to come in and distract me. I'm not going to enjoy this next bit of my life.'

'Like the rest's been just one long party. Wig's good.'

Megan gave her head a shake, fanning the silver wig across her face in a movement she'd tried out on Gemma and the Twins. She'd even got herself a pink one, as Kipper had suggested.

'I've got loads. I can be different every day if I want to.' She climbed on to the bed to give Jackson

140

her chair. He didn't sit down, but propped himself against the door frame. 'Want to see the red one? Mum says I look like a lollipop in it.'

'Megan Bright, Megan Silver,' he said in a singsong way. 'No, that's the one for me. Does she forgive me for trying to scalp you?'

'*She* has. Don't know about Sister Brewster.'

'I'm out of jail for that. Took a while, though. I'll have to do something else very bad and see what happens.'

Megan narrowed her eyes. 'What? You've done everything there is. If I believe what you tell me. Not that I do, half the time.'

Jackson put on a wounded face. 'Nope, there's got to be something . . .'

'You're in hospital, remember?'

'And you think that's going to stop me . . . ?'

She had to concede that it probably wouldn't. Jackson was gazing at her, smiling.

'What?'

'Well . . .' he sat down on the bed. 'Shove over, Wig Girl. Sometimes I jus' have to lay me down . . .'

'Not here you can't.' Megan shot a glance at the door.

Jackson was stretching out on her bed, as if it were his own, though it seemed even more like a baby bed, he was so tall. He kicked off his sandals, laid his head back on her pillow, and tugged his hat over his face.

'Why not?' he said.

141

'Because . . .' Megan pulled up his hat so that she could see him. 'Because . . .' He was grinning at her. The hat dropped back down. 'Oh, never mind.'

She shoved over.

The bed was an island. All about them were sharks and things that chomp on bones. There were storms, and heat which dried you out till plates of skin dropped off and there was nothing to drink. Or so Jackson said.

'I like it here,' he added. 'Much better than a ward. I might just stay for ever. This is a place for stories.'

Footsteps approached, then passed her door. Megan tried to work out who they belonged to but couldn't. It didn't matter.

'Want to hear one?' Jackson said.

'Do I look like a nine-year-old?'

'It'll be good, promise. And I need to practise on you.' Jackson rolled over and lobbed his hat on to the chair. His face was close to hers. He was looking straight at her, as if he remembered another time, in the darkness of the visitors' waiting room, and might want to kiss her again.

She swallowed. 'Go on, then.'

He lay on his back again. There were a few seconds of silence, as if he was preparing himself, gazing into the distance as if another world lay there. 'There was a famine in the land,' he began slowly, lowering his voice, making it sound much, much older, deeper, yet lilting like the tune from a song Megan had never heard before. 'And for months, no rain.' He raised his eyes as if searching for clouds, praying for rain.

Where did he get that voice? Making him sound so different – someone from another place, another time. This wasn't the boy she knew. This was an old man from somewhere back in history. How did he do that?

'Day after day, the sun burn in the cloudless skies.' Jackson raised his hand to the ceiling, made a sun of it. 'The grass parch, like a coffee berry.'

Coffee berry? What was one of those? Like the beans they grind in cafés?

'The trees also parch, and brown, same way, the plants in the trees start to wither away.' His hand became a tree, dying, shrivelling up, with no water to drink. 'There was a famine in the land.' He sat up straight and stopped.

Megan beamed at him. 'How d'you do that?'

Jackson gave her a sheepish smile. 'Just listen, just copy,' he answered, in that slow, old way. He went back to his usual voice. 'I'm trying to sound the way it would in Jamaica, around the fire, at night. No TV, no radio, just stories, under the stars.' He looked once more at the ceiling as if it were sky, then he grinned and the spell was broken. 'Mum says that's how it would've been. Probably, anyway. If Jackson T. Dawes was still alive, he would've known.' Jackson let out a small laugh. Wistful almost. 'Bet he was full of stories.'

'Do you know them off by heart, the ones you tell?'

'Yeah, or I make bits up. As long as it gets to the end. I tell them in a pub near us. Sunday afternoons. They light candles and get it all atmospheric and everything. And there's these kids who just love listening.'

'Are you not going to finish?' Wanting to hear him again, wanting the magic of the sound. Feeling like a kid.

'I'm just learning it. It's hard to keep the accent all the way through a long story.'

'In that case, you have to go,' Megan said, leaning up on her arm.

A frown. 'Why?'

'We're going to be in trouble if anyone walks in.'

Jackson's face lit up. 'Good. I like trouble.'

'But you're not going to finish the story,' she insisted, 'so there's no good reason for you to be here, getting into trouble.'

Jackson sighed. 'You're right. None whatsoever, Wig Girl.' He took a handful of silver hair, pulled it towards him and smiled right into her eyes, so that all she could see were the lights in them, lazy and bright and just for her. Then he dropped his gaze, leaned over so that his head almost touched hers, and brought the hair to his lips, before letting the gleaming strands slowly drift from his fingers.

'I like this,' he said, picking up some more. 'Megan Silver, Megan Bright.'

He was so close she could breathe in the smell of him, the soap, the shower-gel fragrance.

Just outside, the ward was doing what the ward did. The machines clicking on and off, phones ringing and being answered, babies crying and being shushed, mothers lying tired on their children's beds, draped gently around them, because they didn't want to leave them alone. Everything the same as always outside her room, with nurses walking past her open door, too busy to think about what was happening inside.

'We're going to be in trouble,' she said at last.

'Again?' Jackson sighed in a dramatic sort of way, propped himself up on his arm and looked down at her once more. 'But nobody's paying any attention,' he went on. 'What's the point of breaking all the rules if no one catches you at it?'

Megan turned to look at him, at his face, his lips, taking in the smoothness of his head, the gleaming skin, wanting to trail her fingers over him, yet not wanting to in case it would make the dream go away.

'I think something spectacular is called for. So . . .' Jackson began to tug at the fastener on his jeans. 'Now, this is going to bring them running in!'

'What're you doing?' Megan shrieked, jumping off the bed. This was no dream. 'Stop it! Stop it!'

Jackson burst out laughing. 'It's all right, Wig Girl. I'm not that daft. Neither are you.'

Megan flopped down into her chair and began to

laugh till she was almost weak with it. She stopped when she noticed Jackson gazing at her and was caught like a rabbit in the headlights of a car, suspended in the moment, with nothing before, nothing beyond, just waiting, wanting to be trapped for ever in it.

'Another time,' Jackson said. 'Another place. And it would be perfect.'

Megan looked away. Feeling her cheeks burn. Yes. Perfect.

'Got anything to eat? I'm starved.'

'What?' Megan blinked, confused. Did he never settle, was he never still? Was this all just a joke with him? 'In there.'

Jackson made his way around to her locker, but it seemed to take a lot of effort. He stumbled, catching his drip stand on the leg of her bed.

'Watch out!' Megan cried, as if he was about to fall.

He gave her a look she'd not seen before, a look which said, *Don't fuss, I'm fine*. He began to rummage through her things. 'No. Nothing here. Never mind; I'm not supposed to have anything to eat, anyway.'

Megan caught her breath. 'What?'

'You're not the only one going for an operation. I'm having one this afternoon.'

'Jackson, stop messing about.' She tried to sound as if this was just another of his jokes, but when she saw his face, she knew. 'Are you? Really?'

146

'Two o'clock.'

'I'd have just let you eat anything you wanted. Why didn't you say something before?' He was grinning at her. 'It's not funny.'

'Guess what I did this morning before Rooster arrived?' Megan refused to acknowledge him. He dropped his voice. 'Found the mortuary. Full of stiffs. All in fridges.'

'You watch too much telly.'

'Have it your own way.' Jackson glanced at the window and frowned.

'What now?'

Jackson lowered his voice once more. 'The sun done gone away, the storm's coming to the land.' He grabbed his hat, gestured to the window with it and left.

Megan glanced at the sky. It was a solid grey slab, full of rain.

Twelve

It seemed like hours since Jackson went down for his operation. For a time Megan sat on her bed, trying to draw, but nothing would come. Her mobile chimed. Gemma sent her a whole line of ☺s ready for the next day, and the Twins told her to check out the surgeon. He might be nice.

They still didn't know about Jackson. Megan hadn't told them. She couldn't decide why, but every time she thought about saying anything, the words just seemed to dry up. Right now, she was glad they didn't know. The Twins would be sending never-ending texts and she'd have to send never-ending answers.

Megan checked the time. She listened to some tunes on her iPod. She tried on all her wigs, settling for the silver one again. It didn't bring Jackson back to the ward any quicker.

Mum popped in with some cards from various relatives and friends. They went through them together, but Megan couldn't concentrate, hardly seeing the names, hardly reading the messages. She sent Mum away, ignoring the fact that she hadn't been there an hour, ignoring the fact that she looked hurt, and wandered down to Jackson's room, standing there for what seemed like for ever, willing him to come back.

'He'll be away for quite a bit, Megan.' Sister Brewster had appeared at her side suddenly, gentle but firm. 'Come on, now.'

Her own room was no comfort. Right then she hated it, hated the confinement of it. She listened to the rain as it thundered against the window pane, watched it sheeting down the glass, watched great grey puddles, like lakes, grow on the flat roofs.

Why was everything taking so long? He should have been back before now, shouldn't he?

Wandering up and down the corridor later, Megan was aimless as litter. It was a busy day on the ward, with new children coming in, fretful and disoriented, their parents wandering about in a lost, shocked sort of way. Someone new was in Kipper's bed.

She needed to escape. 'Can I go down to the shop? I want to get a magazine,' she said, marching straight to the Nurses' Station, which was milling with staff.

Sister Brewster looked up from the computer in the corner. 'Of course you can, Megan. Just don't go wandering off to places you shouldn't. The operating theatre is strictly out of bounds, as you know, and so is the Recovery Room, which is where Jackson is now.' She gave her a secretive sort of smile.

Megan's eyes filled, but her heart gave a leap of joy. 'He's finished?'

'Yes,' Sister Brewster said, 'but there's a while to go yet. Off you go.'

The shop was on the bottom floor, not far from the main entrance to St Peregrine's. It was a small place with two or three circular tables. Huddled around one sat a mother and her two children. The woman stared into her cup, hair resting limply on her shoulders, fingernails bitten right down. The children, twin boys, sucked away at bottles of juice, having some kind of battle, nudging at each other with their feet, under the table exchanging sly looks.

'Stop that, now,' their mother hissed. 'Or you'll not get those sweets.'

A third child lay grizzling in a buggy pushed in beside them. She was sucking at a huge dummy, like Maggie Simpson, her eyes closed, nose wet. Now and then her fist came up to rub at her face, causing it to screw up into an ugly mask.

As Megan walked past, both boys stopped and gazed at her, wide-eyed. Their mother turned to see why. Megan gave her a grin, shook her head so that the silver wig fanned out around her.

'Don't stare,' the mother commanded; words like bullets. 'Drink your juice.'

The assistant behind the counter smiled at Megan, eyes crinkling behind thick glasses. A string of pearls sat around her neck, making her look like the Queen. 'Oooh, I love the silver. Like a Christmas fairy. Where's your friend?' she said. 'He's not been down today.'

'Having an operation.'

The assistant's face fell. 'Oh, I didn't know.' Her cheeks flushed. 'Poor thing. We've missed him. Regular as clockwork, he is.'

'He's out now,' Megan rushed on, reassuring her. 'He's in Recovery. It won't be long before he comes back up.'

The smile returned. 'That's good. He'll be on his feet in no time. Say we're all asking after him.' A man arrived at the counter. He was holding a large bag of toffee eclairs and a newspaper. The assistant held out her hand for his money. 'Can I get those for you, dear? Terrible day, isn't it? All that rain.' There was a note of relief in her voice. It seemed that terrible weather was a far safer topic than Jackson being in Recovery.

Megan made her way past the revolving card stand, the fridge full of fruit snacks and milkshakes, to the rear wall, with its comics, magazines and newspapers. She glanced occasionally through the large windows into the corridor, to see who was outside, knowing that Jackson could be on his way back. He might come past the shop. But he didn't. Disappointed, she returned to the counter and paid for her magazine.

'Is he not back yet?' Megan could see that Jackson wasn't, she could see that his room was empty, but somehow she couldn't stop herself asking. Maybe they'd put him somewhere else.

Siobhan grinned. 'Megan, you're like a plague with all your questions.'

'So, he's not back.'

'I promise you'll be the first to know. But for now you'll just have to sit and wait.'

Megan's mobile hummed. She took it back to her room. 'Grandad?'

'Just thought I'd give you a ring, see how things are on that ward of yours.'

His voice was tinny as usual. It was the voice of a frail man, someone who hardly got out of bed because of weakness. Only that wasn't Grandad at all. He went out every day to the harbour to talk to the fishermen, to watch the seagulls, to make his lists of birds in his little black notebook. Nobody believed he was in his nineties. Today, though, he sounded just a little bit older.

'Is Mrs Lemon there?' Megan said.

'She's out at the shops. She says I'm not to get into any trouble while she's gone. So I rang you. Big day tomorrow, hey?'

'Jackson's having an operation,' Megan said, not wanting to talk about having her head cut open, not wanting to worry Grandad, when he was all on his own. 'He's been down ages.'

'Oh . . . well . . . You'll see him soon, I'm sure,' Grandad said. 'Don't worry, Pet Lamb. He sounds like a big strong lad. And that *Shee-vorn* will take care of him, right enough.'

Rain drummed against the windows, filling the children's ward with noise. All the lights were on even though it was the middle of the day. Grandad's voice was buried in the sound and seemed planets away. Megan could see him grasping the phone, like an unexploded bomb, and no Mrs Lemon to keep him right. She should try to get him to ring off. But he was still talking, though his voice was sounding more and more faint.

'I might have to go, Grandad. Jackson's probably coming back soon.'

'Aye, off you go, see to that lad. Say hello. And look after yourself. We'll be thinking about you . . . tomorrow . . .'

There was a pause and Megan realised that Grandad was crying, that he couldn't speak because of it.

'I'll be fine, Grandad. And soon as I can, I'll ring you.'

154

'Pet Lamb,' he said.

'Put the phone down, Grandad. And fill the kettle for Mrs Lemon coming back. You know how she likes her cup of tea. Tell her I said hello.'

At last Grandad rang off, but Megan couldn't settle. She went back to Jackson's room, sat behind the door, where no one could see her. The place looked huge with no bed in it. All that remained of him was a tissue, which lay crumpled next to his locker. She picked it up and dropped it into the rubbish bin, unable to bear the thought that he might come back to a messy room.

Megan sat in Jackson's chair, in the hollow that he'd made, so that it held her, hugging her whole body. She laid her hands on the armrests where his fingers sometimes tapped out a tune, found herself pecking at the wood with her nails. She breathed, slowly and deeply, the air Jackson had breathed that very morning. She could almost feel him there in the room, as if he'd left some part of himself behind, just for her.

A siren cut through the air. Megan glanced at the window. It was an ambulance, coming in to the Accident and Emergency Department. Jackson had some story about wandering in there one day, and a nurse herding him back out. Megan imagined what would be happening now, pictured a person being carried in on a stretcher, the doctors and nurses flitting about, doing what they do to save a life. The drips, the cardiac monitoring, the blood transfusions, electric-shock treatment. Just like TV.

When at last she heard them pushing Jackson down the corridor, Megan ran out to see him, pressing back against the wall as he went past. He seemed to be asleep, though a low groan came from him as they swung his bed towards the door.

'Another time, Megan,' someone said in all the bustle of getting him back into his room, opening both doors, manoeuvring things. 'Off you go, for now.'

Later, Megan watched from the doorway as Siobhan moved quietly around Jackson's bed. Temperature. Pulse. Blood pressure. Fluid charts. Intravenous therapy. She was so familiar with all the words; it was like a new language learned.

'He doesn't look very well,' she said, trying not to cry.

'Ach, nobody does after a big operation, Megan. Don't worry.'

Jackson was having a transfusion. There was a steady drip, drip of blood from a bag into the see-through chamber, which was long like a small, stretched balloon, always half full, always half empty. A giving set, they called it. Each new drop into the chamber pushed another down the see-through tubing into Jackson. Megan watched as one oozed and grew into a small red berry before it fell.

'Will he have some more?' she asked Siobhan,

who was now checking the flow, making marks on a chart.

'I think so,' the nurse said, smiling. 'Another unit, I imagine. Well, miss, that's enough for now. When he wakes up later, you can pop in for a few minutes, so you can.'

'Have I got to wait in my room?'

'Anywhere but here, at the moment. Go on. Off with you!'

But Siobhan smiled and Megan knew that she wasn't in trouble, just in the way.

Later, the ward was quiet. Jackson's family had left for the night but he was awake, Siobhan told her. 'You can have five minutes. That's all. He's still drowsy.'

'Five minutes,' Megan promised, making her way quickly to his room, not wanting to waste a second. She stopped in the doorway, not sure if he'd fallen asleep already. The room was lit only from the light above his bed which dropped a halo of gold on to his face.

'Hi.' Jackson's voice sounded crusty, but he managed a weak smile.

'Hiya.' The air was filled with the blinking of a monitor, the click of the drip, and Jackson breathing slowly. 'Are you all right?'

'Can't . . . feel . . . anything.'

'Good. That's good, isn't it?'

Jackson made a slight movement of his head, as if it was too heavy to nod or shake.

'Are you too tired? I'll come back tomorrow. They said I can only stay five minutes.'

'Should've told you . . . something . . .' Jackson shifted his hand just a little towards her, as if he didn't want her to go. His fingers were long and slim, like a musician's, his palm pale, smooth-looking.

'What's that?'

'About Kipper . . .' There was a moment of not knowing what to do, a second of not being sure, then Megan laid her hand over his, afraid she might hurt him. Her fingers rested on his wrist, her palm pressed lightly into his. She could feel his pulse beating against her skin. Jackson swallowed. It looked painful, as if his throat was raw.

'What about Kipper?'

'. . . she died.'

Megan nodded. 'I thought she might have.'

She didn't ask how he knew – of course he would know, the Pied Piper of Hamelin, leading all the children on a Mr Henry hunt, of course he would. She didn't even wonder at how she'd almost felt it would happen when Kipper went home that day to see her kitten, to give him a cuddle. And now it felt so long ago, and far away, like something from another time.

'But she'll still be keeping an eye on Brian.'

'Yes.' Jackson's fingers curled sleepily, lazily, but didn't let her go. 'Better watch out, Brian. No more . . . climbing . . . trees . . .'

Megan sat watching a scarlet berry as it formed in

the drip, following the drop as it sank into the small red ocean that would make its slow way round Jackson's body. Drop by drop, beat by beat. Keeping him safe.

Jackson's hand relaxed into drowsiness. Megan watched his face as it too melted into sleep. She watched and watched until his breathing grew deeper and slower.

His lips looked dry, cracked. They might be sore when he woke.

Gently slipping her hand from his, she found the little tin of vaseline in her pocket, squeezed off the lid and dipped in her finger. She brushed a thin film of balm across Jackson's lips, his smiling, story-telling mouth, now silent, now still, yet moving, as if his flesh were glued to hers for that moment and for all the moments.

She would have stroked his face too, every bit of it; she would have run her fingers over his head, over the joins in his skull, the lines and ridges, so clear beneath his skin; she would have trailed them over his brow and his closed eyes, over his cheek-bones, so fine, so prominent an artist might have drawn them, a sculptor might have chiselled them; she would have laid down on the bed next to him, if it would stop anything else hurting him.

Megan stood up, content to leave him now, but pressed her fingers to him, one last time, kissing them gently against his lips.

She moved away at last.

Her fingertips glistened. She gazed at them under the light from the lamp above Jackson's bed, as if they weren't her own fingers at all, as if they didn't really belong to her. She brought them to her mouth, resting them on her lips, and tasted those remnants of balm, those tiny traces of Jackson, like kisses, still on her skin.

Thirteen

Megan believed in miracles. Sometimes when you least expect it they just happen, she reckoned. Sometimes she prayed for them, though not the way Mrs Lemon did, with rosary beads, or lighting little candles in church.

The miracle she most wanted, right now, would be for her to get down to Theatre and for the surgeon to find her tumour all gone. But if that wasn't possible, then just to see Jackson before she went.

Only that didn't seem to be possible.

He couldn't come to see her. She wasn't allowed to see him. It was too early, he was still asleep, still feeling poorly after his operation.

There were too many reasons. Siobhan said that

she could wave at him as she passed his room, would that be OK?

It wasn't. She'd finished her picture of him last night, staying up late until it was done. She wanted to show him before she went for her operation.

And somehow she got herself into *such a state*, as Siobhan said, that they had to give her something to settle her down. It made her full of wooze, full of clouds, and her words came out like glue.

'Canhenot comehere?' Megan begged again.

'He's got to stay in bed. He had a big operation yesterday.'

'ButIwannaseehim.'

Siobhan patted her hand. 'I know you do, but there are . . . other pebbles on the beach, so . . .' Megan looked up, though it was hard. Siobhan was being so mysterious, with that smile on her face, talking about pebbles and everything. 'And one of them is right here. To see you. A real surprise visitor.' She stepped aside and there he was, right next to her bed.

'Dad?'

Megan had to check, to be completely sure, had to focus her eyes to get him all in. There he was, tanned, dark even, against his white shirt, smiling at her. His eyes still blue, hair still grey and thin, his middle still round, cuddly.

But he shouldn't be here.

'AmIgoingtodie?'

162

Suddenly Megan was convinced that she was. People did with cancer sometimes. Look what happened to Kipper. That's why Dad was here. It had to be the reason why he was here.

'Course not, silly billy.' He leaned over and dropped a kiss on her forehead.

'Where's Mum?'

'Just behind me, see?'

There she was, smiling as if it was a party, not an hour or so before Megan had to have her head cut open. 'Hello, love. This is a nice surprise, isn't it? Having *him* here.'

Megan frowned, then looked at Dad. 'Butwhy're-youhere? Toldyounottocome.'

'Because you're having an *operation*. I've not worked every hour God sends not to be able to come home for that! And Grandad's not here to check they do it right, so it's down to me.' He gave a little laugh. 'I would have come last night, but the flight home was hours late.' He hung up his jacket. 'You don't really mind me being here, do you?'

She'd made him promise not to come but now he was here. It wasn't right . . . and yet . . .

'Notgoingtodie?'

'No. Definitely not.' Dad sounded very sure.

'WillyoubeherewhenIcomeback?'

He sat down next to the bed and gently nudged her arm. 'Just let them try and stop me. I'll be wait-ing here for as long as it takes. Me and Mum.'

'Howlongwillittake?' There was a hesitation. Megan gazed up to see Dad brushing something out of his eyes.

Mum answered. 'A few hours maybe.'

'But you . . .' Dad gave her another nudge, 'will think it only lasted a minute. Honestly. You won't know a thing about it till you wake up.'

Megan closed her eyes. It was easier than trying to keep them open, but all of a sudden tears began to ooze out of them and there was no way to stop it happening. Maybe it was relief at seeing Dad, maybe fear of the operation, but she was helpless.

'Now then, sweetheart. Don't worry.'

Dad found a tissue and dabbed it at her eyes, but Megan couldn't stop. Tears drained down her cheeks, on to her pillow, seeping through to the plastic cover under the pillowcase. They streamed into her ears. It was like a tap turned on full.

'They know where the tumour is,' Mum said, 'and the operation's going to take a bit of time . . . but it isn't over-complicated . . . They'll make sure you'll have plenty of stuff to keep you comfortable afterwards, stop you hurting.'

Dad's voice came, gentle, persistent. 'Injections, into your tube. Probably. That's what you'll have. They won't let you hurt.'

The words weren't helping because it was out of her hands, this crying. Mum squeezed her hand. 'It'll be fine, love.'

'Come on, give us a hug,' Dad said. 'And as soon as you're back on the ward, we'll ring Grandad. He says he'll wait by the phone.'

Notes and X-rays were balanced on her stomach. They felt heavy, solid. Siobhan was there, and Mum, with her arm through Dad's. Everyone looked upside down. The ceiling drifted past. They were going along a corridor. The man pushing the trolley was chatting to Mum and Dad. He said he was from Poland. Sounded like that footballer. Who was it? She shifted her head to see the man from Poland, but he was upside down like everyone else. That couldn't be right.

Pictures. Poppies in fields. Landscapes. A child with big dewy eyes. A horse. Signs for places Jackson would have gone. They all sailed slowly past her. Mum and Dad were talking to her now. Saying it wouldn't be long before she'd be coming back up the corridor. Then a turn, and through two doors.

'Dad?'

'I'm here, sweetie. And Mum. We can come with you till you get the anaesthetic.'

'Thassgood.'

They were in a room. All glass cupboards, all lights and full of people in green.

'Hello. Megan, isn't it? Do you remember me? Dr Singh. I'm the anaesthetist. I came to see you on the ward. Do you remember?' She had a high voice full of

165

laughter, full of smiles. There was a red mark in the middle of her forehead.

'Yesss,' Megan answered.

'Now then, dear, I'm going to put this needle in your hand and give you something to make you go fast to sleep.'

'We'll just be waiting outside,' Mum said, her voice a whisper, like a secret just for her. 'Just outside that door. Once you go to sleep. We'll be there, me and Dad, and you'll see us in no time.'

'Yessss,' Megan said.

'Now, dear, I'm putting the needle in, just a little scratch.' Just a little scratch. There was a click, a snap.

A nurse came over with a syringe full of something milky-looking. She smiled at Megan who blinked up at her but couldn't make her mouth move.

'Now,' the anaesthetist said. 'I want you to count to ten for me. Will you do that, dear? Count for me now. One . . . two . . .'

'Three . . .'

Cool fingers on her wrist, just sitting there, gently. A slight pressure. 'Pulse eighty-four.'

Something on her arm, a hiss and a wheeze, growing tighter until her hand ached and all the blood stopped. Then slowly back, thump, thump, thump. Another hiss and the tightness disappeared.

'BP a hundred over sixty.'

Awake. Almost. Asleep. Almost. A drowsy delicious

in-between thing drifting around like mist. She couldn't catch it. Nothing belonged. Sleep came but wouldn't stay. She wanted it to stay, wanted to keep her eyes closed, to stop them shivering open, but sleep went away again, wakefulness came.

Words. All around her. She recognised them but not the voices.

Where was she? Ah, what did it matter? It was a nice feeling, this. In and out of clouds and sleep and waves and warmth.

Lovely. Lovely.

She half opened her eyes to see the lights hanging in strips above her. Too bright. Eyes closed again. The lights stayed there like pictures.

Something around her head. A band. She couldn't feel her ears. Maybe they'd gone away, somewhere else. No, that wasn't right.

'Megan . . . hello, Megan. Time to wake up.' A warm hand took hold of hers. 'Come on. Open your eyes, Megan.'

She tried but they were glued shut.

'Squeeze my hand. Come on.'

Squeeze.

'And again, come on.'

Squeeze again.

'She's fine. You can take her back to the ward.'

All a dream. Just a dream.

But there was Dad.

A miracle.

Fourteen

Megan remembered nothing about the time after her operation. It was just a blank space. She'd been very ill, spiked a fever they told her later, showing her the temperature chart, the line shooting up like an arrow to the sky. It was touch and go, they said, really touch and go.

It wasn't until the line began to make its jittery way down the chart that Megan began to feel better and the blank space began to fill up with words, only they were like random pieces of a puzzle, all there but in no order at all. It took for ever to sort it out, and when it was complete, Jackson wasn't there. Neither was Siobhan or Sister Brewster. Where were they all? The questions tumbled about in her head. *Where am I? Am I in the right place?*

All around her were strange nurses, checking her, tidying her, washing and drying her, because she could hardly lift a finger to help herself.

When, finally, she was able to sit up, all shaky and weak, she was in her old room and there was talk of going home, that being the best place, now that her operation was all over and she was on the mend. But she didn't want to go home, not if Jackson was coming back.

She had to see him.

Relentlessly, the days moved on till it was her last one, and still Jackson wasn't back. Or maybe he was, and they didn't want her to know. That was it. Of course it was. They didn't want them to be together. Someone must have seen them that day in her room. They'd put him on the adult ward to keep them apart.

Megan wandered, a little unsteadily, around the place, looking for Jackson but all she found were children. They were so young. One had a mask over his face attached to the oxygen line behind his bed. He looked very pale, apart from his cheeks, which glowed like small red apples.

There were parents playing with their children, or reading to them, some just holding hands. One boy vomited into a bowl. He looked at the contents in complete surprise. His head was as bald as an egg.

A little girl lay flat on her back with a drip attached to her arm. She was fast asleep. Maybe she'd had an operation. Maybe she was waiting for one. Whatever it was, her mum looked very tired, leaning into the bed, eyes closed, her hair in rats' tails.

There was the octopus, sitting in the corner. There were the dolphins, swimming up walls. On the windows, pretty starfish, shells, mermaids, sea horses. How hadn't she seen these things before? Maybe she'd been too fed up to notice when she first came in, so long ago.

She wandered past Jackson's old room and found someone else lying in his bed. It was a girl about the same age as him. Somehow that was shocking. The girl turned her head, looked at Megan. She was pale, wispy, her arms like twigs, eyes huge. Her body hardly made a lump under the sheet.

The Nurses' Station. Sister Brewster was there, talking to one of the ward auxiliaries.

'Where's Jackson?' Megan said, interrupting, not caring.

Sister Brewster exchanged a look with the auxiliary who picked up some charts and bustled away with them. 'I was busy talking, Megan. You could see that.'

'Yes, but where is he?' She felt weak now, after all that walking, and wanted to sit down, but she wouldn't. Not till she knew.

Sister Brewster gathered together some pieces of paper, straightening them up as if it was vitally important they be straightened. A young doctor

Megan didn't recognise rushed up to the desk, grabbed a stethoscope and rushed off.

'Forgot this,' he said. 'Hi, Megan. You're looking good! Home today, hey?'

He tore down the ward, not waiting for an answer.

Megan turned back to Sister Brewster, determined to stay until there was an answer. A baby cried a weak little note from a nearby room. Someone shushed it gently.

'He went home, Megan. You know that already. You've asked every single nurse,' Sister Brewster said with a sigh. There was something in her voice now, softness perhaps.

'I thought he had some more treatment to get,' Megan persevered. 'He said he did, before he had his operation.' She stood and waited. Sister Brewster looked down at the papers studying them for a few seconds.

'Yes, that's right, but ... there are some treatments you can have at home. It's a better place really. More comfortable. No restrictions. Most people prefer it, really ...'

Megan waited to hear something about rules, about breaking them, about haircuts, razors, mortuaries, staying up too late. There was nothing. Sister Brewster merely cradled the papers against her chest.

'Will he be coming back?'

'No, Megan, he won't.'

Megan stared down at her slippers. Mum had bought them specially. She hated slippers, hated having to wear them. They made her feel like a baby.

'Is he never coming back?'

'No,' came the reply, gentle, final. 'He isn't.'

But how could that be right? Jackson wouldn't have gone without saying something. He would have said goodbye.

Megan raised her eyes to meet Sister Brewster's. She held them, determined not to look away first, determined to hear a different answer. She didn't care how busy the ward was, she didn't care that somewhere, very close, the weak-sounding baby was still crying and wouldn't be comforted.

She wanted a different answer.

It didn't come.

Fifteen

Dreaming. Everything fuzzy, falling apart. A puppet with no strings. Too early, too dark. Trying to catch hold of something, but it was sliding away.

'Megan, love. I have to get going soon.' Everything a whisper, like secrets. 'Come on, love, up you get. I want to be on the road – soon as the traffic dies down. It'll take me a good two hours.'

Grandad's birthday. Oh no. The party she didn't want to go to. And didn't know how to say it.

Mum's cool hand on her forehead. 'Are you feeling all right?'

How could she ever feel *all right* again? 'Course, Mum. Just forgot to set my alarm.'

It had been a long time since she'd had to.

'You do feel better, don't you?'

It was three months since she'd left hospital. Megan smiled, so that Mum would know she was OK. Keeping bright. Keeping cheerful. Letting her know it was all right. Easy-peasy. 'Stop fussing, Mum.'

Mostly she did feel better. Really. And she was glad to be away from the ward and elephants on curtains, and octopus beanbags and little ones, and Sister Brewster.

Only.

Megan slid her fingers under the pillow . . . just in case . . . just to see if everything was still there. And of course it was. Nothing had *magicked* them away. Nothing could.

Mum opened the curtains and sunlight swept in. She was wearing Dad's dressing gown. Blue towelling. And just a short thing but it swallowed her up, bunching around her waist, making her look fat. Her hair was wet from the shower, her cheeks pink.

Why was she still standing there if everything was such a rush?

'What's wrong?'

'I was just wondering, if you wanted to . . . change your mind about . . . the hospital . . . ? I could make a detour. The new unit's so special and you've been invited.'

Not *this* again.

'Just to say hello. Sister Brewster said she'd love to see you there.'

'Mum!'

'But it's the *opening ceremony*. It's important. There's an MP going, someone from London, and that X Factor person – what's her name? Oh, I can't remember. You know.'

'Mum . . .'

'And the newspapers. TV. It's a big thing.' The words came out in one long line. 'It's on my way and there's a direct bus back here for you. It's a new service.'

Would she never, ever, give up?

'I don't *want* to, Mum. I've told you. Every time you ask. I don't care if it's a stupid opening ceremony. Going on about it's not going to make me change my mind.'

Mum looked frustrated.

She was going to be even more frustrated when she found out that Megan wasn't going to Grandad's either. Upsetting all the careful plans – Mum going on ahead, taking everyone's stuff, while Megan waited for Dad to come home so she could travel down with him.

But . . . one disappointment at a time.

'All right. If that's what you want.' Mum sighed, shook her head.

'It is. You know it is.'

Megan refused to look at her, refused to even look in that direction, not until she could hear the door open, hear it close and know that Mum was on the other side.

177

But she hadn't gone. 'You know, love, I'm here if you want to talk about it . . .'

Megan didn't answer, didn't try to tell Mum the thing she'd been putting off. She just listened for the door to close and Mum's footsteps to pad away.

Under her pillow lay the picture, which she loved, and the letter, which she hated. All folded up into tight little squares. Everything about her squeezed into them. The Megan she once was, back in the hospital. She tried not to think about it. But it was like a pain that nothing could stop and nothing could take away.

'What am I going to do with you?' Mum's voice was ready to snap, like a too tight wire. 'Tell me, because I don't know.' She was standing by the toaster. A black thread of smoke trailed from it and burnt toast shot out. 'Now, look what's happened. And there's no more bread.'

As if it was all *her* fault. Everything wrong in the whole wide world. Megan stood waiting for Mum to get over it, to stop blaming her for burnt toast or make her go anywhere. She was fourteen now, old enough to look after herself. She tried to look sorry for causing so much trouble. She tried to show that she knew how hard everything had been for Mum, what with the cancer and hospital and worrying and everything.

Yet she couldn't. 'I just don't want to go. I know I should have said something before now.'

Mum scraped the toast with quick, hard move-ments. Crumbs sailed into the air then cascaded down into the sink. Tiny black specks freckled the white enamel.

'It would have been *helpful*, yes.' Now the Lurpak, slapped on in layers. More butter than bread. 'Where exactly is it you don't want to go? Grandad's? Or the new unit? Either way, people are going to be disap-pointed. Hurt even. Is that what you want? To hurt people after all they've done for you?'

Jesus, Mum. 'I just don't want to go to a party. Anybody's party. Not even Grandad's.'

'It's his *ninety-sixth birthday*! He might not *see* another one.' Mum crunched into her toast. It exploded into pieces which flew everywhere. 'Oh, for crying out loud!'

Megan took a deep breath and picked up the mess on the table.

Every year it was the same. Grandad might not see another birthday.

Yes, that was true. This could be his last. No one goes on for ever.

Some people hardly go on at all.

'I should never have said you could wait for Dad to get back.' Mum bustled about gathering up a few last things. 'I must have been out of my mind.'

'Gemma's staying,' Megan said, trying to sound convincing.

'I'm leaving it up to your dad. He's not going to want two fourteen-year-olds on their own. Not for a whole week. Word gets round. There'll be all sorts turning up at the door expecting parties and raves.' Mum dumped her case into the boot of the car. The last bag was in. 'It's probably not even legal.'

Mum made a big drama about coming back into the house to check she hadn't forgotten anything. Bag. Keys. Purse. That blue blouse. No, that was already in. And the silver sandals to go with her dress. Birthday present. Flowers for Mrs Lemon. She could easily wait another ten minutes while Megan packed her bag, so that she didn't need to worry about lugging anything down by train . . . all of Dad's stuff was in the car . . .

On and on she went. Megan said nothing.

'I don't know what I'm supposed to tell Grandad. You've always gone to his parties. Since you were born.' Mum was looking at her with complete bewilderment.

If only Megan could explain it better. She didn't feel like partying but it wasn't just that. She gazed down at her feet, at her toes curling into the carpet, the green nail varnish she'd put on just last night. It was smudged round her little toe on one side. It looked a mess.

'He'll understand, won't he? I've been ill. He keeps ringing up to say I should take it easy. Just tell him I'm still not better yet.'

Mum flung her a look. 'You *are* better. They said so at the hospital.' She marched into the living room, over to the alcove by the chimney, pulled out a box and brandished it at her. The box which used to have all the sterile packs, the dressings, the sticky tape, the towel, everything to keep her tube clean and safe when she was at home. The box and its contents, which always reminded her that she'd had cancer.

'Look. See? It's empty. I threw everything out. And now I'm going to flatten this for the recycle.'

Mum punched the box till it collapsed, came back through to the hall and shot into the kitchen, like a bullet ricocheting. She threw the crushed cardboard into the box where everything went until bin day. Swinging round, she faced Megan, her face thunderous. This sudden uncharacteristic anger made Megan flinch.

'You *are* better,' Mum went on. Then, all of a sudden, the fire went out. She slumped down on the chair by the phone, her face full of angry blotches. 'Oh, God! I'm acting like a mad woman.'

Megan's stomach squeezed. 'I'm sorry. I really am. It's just . . .' Oh, why couldn't she explain? Why couldn't Mum see? Yet how could she, when Megan didn't know herself?

'Yes, yes. I know you're sorry.' Mum closed her eyes and blew out a breath. 'And so am I.'

Silence, but for the ticking of the clock from the kitchen. It had a loud tick. The big hand shuddered when it moved, as if time was too heavy to push, as if it knew that to stop would cause all sorts of mayhem, with everyone lost, stranded between the seconds.

Megan didn't know what to do or say, nor did she want Mum driving anywhere when she was upset – something else to be blamed for. There might be a crash or anything.

'Do you want a cup of tea? Before you go?'

Mum sighed and stood up, straightening her clothes as if all that action and temper had wrinkled them. 'No. Thanks. I'm all right now. And I'll stop for coffee halfway there.' She held her arms out in a sort of apologetic way, as if it was all her own fault, this outburst, this unexpected loss of control. Megan walked into them, allowing herself to be pulled in close.

Mum was on her way at last. Megan promised she'd look after Dad when he got back the next day and make sure he had a good night's sleep before getting the train to Grandad's. He'd be no good at a party all jet-lagged.

'And if you do change your mind,' Mum said, 'well, your ticket's there. We can't get it refunded. It would be a waste, really, not to use it.'

Megan ignored this as nicely as she could and said she'd ring Gemma and arrange a time to come over. There was loads of stuff in the freezer to eat. They'd be fine. No need to worry.

Mum had to be satisfied with that and drove off with a wave and a shake of her head, which said, *teenagers, why do they have to be so difficult?* She wasn't to know that Gemma was going to a concert with the Twins and wouldn't be able to stay that night. She wasn't to know that, really, Megan didn't want her to come at all, hadn't even asked her. What was the point?

She only wanted one person.

Dad would have something to say. He always did if Mum made him.

He was soft, though; he was the one made out of jelly, where Mum could be as hard as stone. He was the one who could be melted. It would be OK. Megan would send him to Grandad's without her.

Then she could be alone.

No one fussing, no one telling her what to do now she was better. Look to the present. Look to the future. Get back on track. That's what everyone kept saying. How were you meant to do that, exactly? When the present was just a big black hole inside? When the future was so far away you couldn't see it? When the tracks had been ripped up?

Everything was different now. Gemma didn't fit in, or the Twins. Neither did Grandad. Nobody did. Not Mum, not Dad. It was like being stuck between two worlds, not knowing how to get back, not knowing which one to choose. Not wanting either.

Gemma had rung earlier to see if Megan wanted

to come to the concert. It wasn't a great band or anything, but a few lads from school were in it – they knew them, liked them and everything.

Megan made some vague comment about Grandad's birthday.

'Oh, his party. I forgot.' Gemma knew all about the parties and she'd met him at last, when he'd come to visit Megan between treatments. He'd invited her and the Twins to his next one. 'Wish him happy birthday from me.'

Later Megan stood at the mirror to see if telling so many lies made a person look different. It didn't. She ran her fingers through her spiky brown hair, The scar was still there. Even now she winced as her fingers found it, the fine ridge of it, the curve. It didn't hurt, hadn't hurt for ages, in fact. It was more the thought of it being there, the reason behind its presence. That's what made her shudder.

In the drawer beneath the mirror was a tub of gel. Megan smoothed some of it on to her hair to see what would happen. She frowned. A yard brush. That's what she looked like. All spiked up on top and skinny as a handle, the rest of her.

It wasn't a good look. Not here, outside the hospital, away from the ward.

She ran a bath, both taps turned on, sending waterfalls booming against the green plastic bottom and splashing back up again in clouds of spray. The noise was so loud that even if the phone went she wouldn't be able to hear it, with the door locked, extractor fan on and the shower radio, which gave out more hiss than music, turned up high. The message machine would have to listen to Grandad, if he rang, or Mum, or even Dad, who might want to start the arguing process from some airport in the middle of nowhere.

Let him try. Let him argue with his own voice telling him *We're all busy right now, leave a message, we'll get right back to you.* And let him wait.

She wasn't going to the birthday party.

Megan didn't usually have a bath. That was Mum's thing when she wanted to relax and soak away the troubles of the day, the way they did in adverts – she had a bottle of blue stuff for that very purpose. Megan shook some in. Then some more. Bubbles began to blossom in the waterfall, like galaxies of stars. They became so thick, they buried the sound of the running taps. Steam rose to the ceiling and swam around the room in clouds. It began to dim the mirror tiles above the taps.

Climbing in, Megan sank until all she could see in the mirror was a boa of bubbles around her neck, a beard of them round her chin and dangles of them from her ears. The bath glimmered with sparkling foam and soon her reflection faded away in the steam.

They'd be discussing the party. Mum and Mrs Lemon. Who was coming, who wasn't. Not that they ever knew, until it happened. People from the Care

Home in the village would be going. They'd have had the Special Visit from Grandad to remind them and they'd all have to be showered and powdered and dressed, ready when the day arrived. It was up there with Christmas, Grandad's party.

He called the people from the Care Home the Poor Old Souls, and said things like, *There but for the Grace of God I go . . .* or something. When she was little, Megan thought he was saying *There but for the Grapes of God I go . . .* and didn't really know what he meant – only that it wasn't a good thing. Grandad had never liked grapes. The pips got stuck in his teeth. He still had his own. That was supposed to be good, at his age.

Grandad reckoned that once he scored his century and the Queen sent him her telegram, he was going to give up the parties and have something small in his front room, with glasses of sherry and Battenberg cake, the way the Poor Old Souls did.

By then, he said, he might feel like one of them. But he'd never go into a Care Home. If he ever lost his marbles, he said, or couldn't get down to the harbour, they had to shoot him, like they do horses. He wasn't going into one of 'those places'. He said he'd rather have that echinacea. It was a joke with him. He meant euthanasia. He meant, when life wasn't worth living, he didn't want to live it.

Megan flicked at the bubbles around her toes. Some people didn't get that choice. Some people didn't get the chance to live half as long as Grandad, a quarter.

Less, even.

She got it down to a tenth.

The soapy foam drifted away like slow shoals of gleaming fish, then drifted back again, as if attracted to her skin. The water was cooling. There was no room in the bath to top it up. It was already lapping at the grille around the overflow pipe.

Megan sat up in the bath and found the soap, lathering it up between her hands and as she did so, the bubbles around her began to pop, swathes of them disappearing in a fizz of miniature explosions, as if she'd waved a magic wand at them instead of a bar of yellow soap. The last few bubbles clung on, but not for long. They too disappeared, their tiny lives ending, just like that.

Sixteen

The phone rang and Megan knew it would be Mum. It was time for *EastEnders*. Mrs Lemon would be watching it. Mum hated it, so did Grandad.

'Just checking you're OK.' Mum didn't sound angry any more, or exasperated, just resigned. 'I've told them your news, but Mrs Lemon says there can't be a proper party without you, so can you feel better soon and get yourself here.' There was a chuckle in the background. 'And someone else wants to speak to you . . . here she is, Dad.'

There was a pause when Megan imagined Mum handing the phone to Grandad and him trying to work out which way to hold it up, never having got used to it, even after all this time.

'Hello, Pet Lamb,' he said at last, in that tinny

189

tuneful way of his. Hearing his ancient voice was like drinking a cup of Mrs Lemon's home-made soup, the sort with ham and lentils in it. It made her feel hungry. It made her feel as if the big black hole inside her was growing. It made her eyes sting.

'I'm sorry for not coming, Grandad.'

'I should think you are, when there's so much to do, but it's all right.'

'Is it?'

Grandad gave one his laughs. 'Of course it is, pet. If you don't feel in the party mood, who am I to make you? "We'll always have Paris," won't we?'

He'd never been to Paris, he'd never left the village, what with his gammy leg and not being allowed in the war. He'd never done anything with his life, he said once. But he did like that film. *Casablanca*.

'Always,' Megan said.

'You can come up after the party for a day or two.' Was Mum telling him what to say? Was she standing next to him, prompting him?

'But I have school soon, Grandad, beginning of September.' Only a week and half left.

Another pause, as if he was trying to work out a problem. 'Yes, of course. I forgot about that.' He brightened. It sounded real, not put on. It made Megan chew her lip. Grandad was trying so hard to be positive, trying so hard not to be hurt or worried.

'Back to all your friends and football and everything. Of course! Everything the way it was. That's going to be great, isn't it?'

Her throat tightened. He always sounded as if nothing could get him down for long and he expected the same from everyone else. But how could he know what it felt like? He couldn't. He never would. He might be ninety-six almost but he couldn't know.

Ninety-six. How does a person get to live that long?

'Still there, Pet Lamb?'

'Yes, Grandad. Still here.'

The words were hard to find. She didn't want to speak to someone that old, not right now. She didn't want to celebrate the fact that people could reach almost a hundred and still sound as if they would go on for ever.

When Gemma rang again the next day, she didn't sound normal. 'I thought you were going away? But my mum says she saw you going into the shop this morning. Are you all right?'

She had never said so much in one go. Which could only mean one thing.

Megan paused. More lies to tell. 'I thought I'd wait till Dad got home. Go with him.' The clock began to chime. 'He should be home soon. We're going tomorrow.'

'Oh. You didn't say. When I rang, I thought you would have told me.'

191

'I only decided yesterday.'

'You could have come to the concert with us, then. You could have stayed. Mum wouldn't mind. She'd love to see you. Do you want to come round now?'

And do what exactly? Same old stuff they used to do? Like nothing had happened. Like everything was the same? Swapping clothes? Straightening hair? Trying out make-up? The problem page? Talking about boys? Nothing was going to be the same, ever again.

'Can't. Dad'll be home soon.'

'Will I come round there, then? Till he comes?'

Gemma was hurt. That's what all this was about. She didn't stamp about and cry the way the Twins did if they were upset. She did it quietly, like everything else, and she didn't accuse people or judge them and she was fair and sorted out everyone's problems because she listened. But it showed in her face. In her eyes and in her mouth. And, Megan realised, in the sound of her voice, the number of words she used.

'He'll not be long. I've got to go now.'

Gemma wasn't having any. 'Are we not friends any more?' There it was. Just a slight tremor, hardly there, if you didn't know her. They'd been friends since junior school. Since they were eight, when Gemma was new and didn't know anyone.

'Yeah. Course we are.' Megan sighed. Go away. Leave me alone. Dad'll be home soon and he's not going to be very happy with me and I can only deal with one problem at a time.

'Well, it doesn't feel like it. It's like you don't want anything to do with me or the Twins.' There was a pause. 'I know you've been ill and it's been horrible and everything. And I don't know what it was like. But I've missed you. And you never ring me. Or text. It's always me. And I'm sorry I didn't come in to see you but . . .'

'You were busy . . . It doesn't matter. The hospital's too far away, anyway. I know.'

'Well, yes, all of that. School and everything. But it does matter . . . And I was frightened.' Gemma was crying now. 'And I didn't know what to say. Or do. Or ask. I got a book about it, but I couldn't even read it. And I looked it up on the internet and there was all this stuff and photographs of kids and stuff, dying and everything and . . .'

You can get a book about your friend having cancer? Maybe she should read it and find out how it's meant to work.

'Well, I'm still here,' Megan said, though it felt like the biggest lie of all. She was here and not here.

A car rolled up outside. Could be a taxi. Voices now. Could be anyone.

'It's all right, Gemma. Honestly. I've got to go. Dad's here now.'

Maybe it was a lie. Maybe not.

Seventeen

Dad sat like a big cat yawning and stretching and all slumpy in his chair. He'd had a shower and a shave as soon as he got in, which left him looking dark and shiny, like wood, he was so tanned. Sleep was what he needed, but he wouldn't be allowed back upstairs until at least ten o'clock, to get over his jet lag. Mum's orders.

'Lord, you're a hard woman!' he said, yawning again. 'So is your mother. By the way, we have to make sure any mail goes down to Grandad's. Even though we'll be back in a week. Make sure there's a bill or two in there. You know how she likes to worry about bills.'

Megan sat down on the floor with a bundle of stuff which had come earlier and the mail from the day

195

before. 'I've got them here. A whole stack came this morning.' She began to go through them, wondering if Dad already knew about her not wanting to go with him.

The newspapers were there for Dad, in a pile waiting to be read. He liked to look at them and catch up with what was happening in the world, sitting in his own armchair, in his own home. But he wasn't reading anything. He was just sitting and after a while Megan noticed he was looking at her. This was it. This was where he was going to convince her that she needed to go to Grandad's and she was going to have to convince him that she didn't.

'Is it my hair?' she said, playing for time.

'No, it's not that.' Dad clasped his hands. He was going to come out with it. Serious talk. He looked even more tired than before, all of a sudden. Maybe he should just go to bed and sleep right through till morning. 'I heard there was a letter.'

Megan stiffened. Her heart began to thump in swift panicky jolts.

Tell me I have to go to Grandad's.

Make me go. Don't talk about the letter.

And I've told so many lies, don't you want to know about that?

And Gemma hates me. Let's talk about her.

'Mum told me. She was upset, worried, you know. About you.'

The black hole came back and began to grow inside her again. Just as it did with every single memory, with every single hour she remembered of the hospital. And it wouldn't go away. It never did. No matter how hard she tried to put it away. But Dad was still looking at her, as if he wanted an answer, when he already had it, as if he wanted her to remember even though it hurt.

'Yes, there was a letter.'

'I was very sorry to hear about it,' Dad said. 'Very sorry. I wanted to call, but I didn't know what to say. Wanted to see you face to face. But now, I still don't know what to say.'

'It's all right,' she told him. 'I'm fine.'

She gazed down at the mail on the floor. Mainly white envelopes, some brown, with see-through windows filled with black writing, the same name, the same address, the same everything that was on the letter that came before.

It had been addressed to Mum, the hospital stamp making it look horribly official. Megan immediately thought there'd been a mistake, that they hadn't got rid of the tumour after all.

She remembered Mum sitting down and opening the envelope, which revealed another. 'Sister Brewster sent it,' she said, opening the next, complete puzzlement in her voice.

Megan frowned, but even so a sudden hope

197

flickered into life, like a dying candle given air at the very last moment. Of course! Why didn't *she* think to ask Sister Brewster to send a letter? It would have been so simple. 'It's from Jackson, isn't it?'

'It's not from Jackson.' Mum hesitated, reading it. She handed it to Megan. 'It's from one of his sisters. Oh, dear me. I'm so sorry, love.'

And Megan knew.

She knew what the letter would say before she even looked at it; she'd known since Sister Brewster told her that he wasn't coming back to the ward.

How could she not?

After the first few lines, Megan pushed it back at Mum. 'Why don't they just come out with it?'

Mum folded it again and again until it was just a small square. 'Come out with what?'

'That he's dead. Why don't they just say it? He wasn't even sixteen.' Megan spat out the words.

Mum didn't move. 'He's at peace now, love. In a better place.'

'How can you say that?' Megan yelled. 'He should be *here*! *This* is a better place.'

'But they could do nothing for him. It's in the letter, if you'd read it. In the end it's what he wanted.'

Megan had slammed her hand down on the table so that the cups rattled. What did *Mum* know about Jackson? Nothing. Absolutely nothing. 'It's *not* what he wanted. It's not!' she screamed, head hurting, hand stinging. 'He wanted to be a *musician*, he wanted to *live*. He did!' Mum's arms went around her but Megan shook them off. 'It's not fair! How could he do this?'

She raced out of the kitchen, so angry with Jackson that she refused to cry, so furious with him, with Mum, with the whole world, that she swept every single book off her shelves. Bang, bang, bang, they went, slamming one on top of another to the floor. Dust spiralled into the air. Mum ran upstairs.

'Stay out!' Megan yelled, fire blazing somewhere deep within her. 'I don't want you in here. Go away, Mum!' She ran to her door, jamming herself against it. The footsteps halted, and retreated downstairs. Megan shut her eyes, blocking out the sunlight in her room, her breath coming in short bursts, as if she'd run a race. Inside her head she was screaming, the noise so deafening that she couldn't think any more.

'But you see, I don't believe you *are* fine,' Dad said, bringing her back. 'Anything but. And Mum's worried about you.' He sighed. 'It's been hard for her to help . . . when you won't talk about it . . . no one can help.'

Megan couldn't bear to look at him because he'd made her remember and remembering made the fire inside blaze even more. Was that supposed to help? Why was he doing this? The best thing was not to think about it *at all*, could he not see that? Couldn't Mum?

'I only met Jackson once,' Dad went on as if he wanted to torture her, saying Jackson's name like that, as if he were still alive, still breathing and laughing, still holding her hand. 'But I was glad to see the boy you couldn't stop talking about.'

Megan stared at the pile of letters, then realised with a start what Dad had just said.

'You met him . . . ? Jackson?'

Dad frowned, examining his fingers. 'Of course I did,' he said, sounding puzzled. 'He came barging in after your operation, demanding to see you, because he was going home.' Megan froze. 'When I say, barging in, it wasn't exactly like that.'

'He came? To see me?'

'Yes.' Dad was looking at her as if she should know this. 'Siobhan pushed him in. He was in a wheelchair, but that lad was determined.' Dad started to look uncomfortable as if something dreadful was dawning on him. 'Said he had a story to finish. I didn't catch much. You were very ill. I wasn't really concentrating.'

Jackson had been to see her?

That couldn't be right.

Megan's head spun with a thousand thoughts. If he had, *why* hadn't someone said?

Dad carried on. 'I think maybe Jackson knew he mightn't get to see you again . . . that's why he came.' He paused. 'To say goodbye.'

Megan looked at her shoes. They were blurred, out of focus, as if they didn't really belong to her feet. Her throat tightened.

'I didn't know,' she said, her voice almost a squeak. 'No one told me. Why didn't you tell me?' Something huge began to well up inside her.

'Oh, Lord.' He closed his eyes and for a few seconds it seemed he would never talk again. His face looked even more crumpled. 'You were so ill. We . . . thought we were going to lose you . . .' he said, his voice trailing away. 'Oh, God, I'm so sorry. I thought Mum had told you.'

'But I thought he'd just gone off . . . without saying anything . . . All this time, I've been thinking . . .' She was about to explode, like thunder.

Dad eased himself off the sofa, down on to the floor beside her. 'I don't know what to say, love. I really don't.' Megan couldn't look at him. 'And I know it's a shock, but now you know, maybe you can . . .'

'Don't tell me to move on. Don't tell me to celebrate his life.' Megan said, her voice level, cold. 'Just don't. That's what they all say.'

Nodding slowly, Dad put his arm lightly around her shoulders. Megan could feel his strength, his warmth. 'I'm not going to.'

'He's dead.' The words felt like pieces of stone in her heart. 'There's nothing to celebrate.'

'There is, you know,' Dad leaned towards her.

Megan shook her head, suddenly and completely miserable. 'The fact that Jackson could make you feel this way tells me he was a fantastic young man.' Megan stared at Dad's shoes, the pattern of tiny holes in the leather, the double knot he always tied them with, the polished gleam of them. 'He made you happy, I know he did. Helped you through. And Grandad thought the world of him because of it.' But Jackson was gone, that's all Megan knew. 'And he was strong enough to fight all the way,' Dad went on. 'And that's what's great about him. That's what you *could* celebrate.'

'I can't.' Megan's throat filled, her eyes filled, everything so full to bursting.

Dad pulled her to him. 'It's not running around with balloons and shrieking and dancing. It's not like the party Grandad's going to have.' It was all Megan could do to breathe, yet crying seemed easy, and now it was the only thing she could do, weeks of crying all at once. 'Remembering the good times you had with him, love, that's what I'm talking about.' Dad's voice broke through.

'Don't know how,' Megan wailed. 'I can't do it.'

'You can. You will,' Dad said, his voice solid. 'You had good times with him, didn't you?' Megan nodded into his shoulder. 'Remembering them and having a smile. That's what I mean about celebrating.' Dad eased Megan away from him, his warm hands clasped around her shoulders. He looked deeply into her eyes. 'Oh, love, one day you will, I promise. One day you will celebrate.' Then pulling her to him once more, he held Megan as if he would never let her go.

Eighteen

'Well, hello, stranger!' Sister Brewster towered above Megan, hands on hips appraising her from top to toe. She sounded amazed, looked it too, for a brief moment, then it was back to the same Sister Brewster. 'You missed the opening ceremony,' she said. 'The new unit?'

Megan ignored this and handed over the present she'd brought with her, still not sure why she'd decided to come; even now her stomach was churning, her hands trembling. But she'd stay just for a minute, that's all. 'These are for you.'

'Mmmm, lovely. That's really kind, but you gave us lots when you went home, remember.'

'They'll all be gone now and nurses love chocolates. Besides, Mum sent them.' Another lie, but she didn't care. 'These are from me.' Megan held out a plastic bag. 'For the new place. If you want them. If you're allowed.' There were half a dozen of her own CDs and DVDs. 'They're not new or anything.'

'That's so kind, Megan, really it is.' Sister Brewster took them out and examined them. 'These are great. Thank you.' She laid them aside and clasped her hands together. 'But we wanted you to come to the opening. As our special guest. Why didn't you?'

Megan swallowed. You *know* why, she wanted to say. But the words wouldn't come.

Sister Brewster looked at Megan with those big eyes, trapping her almost, as if there was much more to say, much more to hear. But this was a busy ward, she would have lots to do. Even now there was the wail of a baby, the shriek of a toddler. Maybe she should go.

'Would you like to see the unit, now that you're here?' Meeting her gaze, Megan saw something supremely warm and kind in it just for her.

Megan tried to smile. 'I can't stay long. Dad's at home. We're . . . meant to be going to Grandad's today. He doesn't know I've come. I mean, he's all jet-lagged and sleeping. I didn't want to disturb him.'

'So, is that a yes or a no?'

'Have you got time?'

'Of course, I have. But hang on just a second.' Sister Brewster went off, leaving Megan by the Nurses' Station. There was a tap on her shoulder.

'Well, now! And who's this?'

'Siobhan!'

One big hug later they were both grinning.

'You look *great*! Told you, didn't I?' Siobhan sounded delighted. 'How's everything else?'

Such a small question, just a few words, but the answer was too huge to give.

'Grandad's ninety-six on Sunday. He's having a party.'

Siobhan smiled. 'Ninety-six! That's a fantastic age!'

'Yes, it is,' Megan said, almost puzzled by how proud she suddenly felt to have a grandfather that old.

Siobhan squeezed her arm. 'And back to school for you! That'll be great, won't it?'

Megan nodded because it seemed that Siobhan wanted it to be so. Sister Brewster came up, handed over a bunch of keys and exchanged a few quiet words at the desk.

'Off to the unit, hey?' Siobhan said. 'You'll love it! Got to go. Keep in touch!'

Sister Brewster strode down towards the ward doors, unlocking them. It was a quick march down the main corridor, a turn to the right and down another corridor. Sister Brewster's black shoes squeaked as she walked.

'You have to be at least thirteen to get anywhere near this place, mind you. No screaming babies or annoying toddlers, no elephants, no octopus, and no Disney characters. *Especially* no Disney characters.'

Megan grinned, embarrassed. The number of times she'd complained . . .

'It has a pool table. There's table tennis, a sitting room, music room, quiet room, you name it room. And anyone who stays has to suggest ways of making it better. There's a box for comments.' Sister Brewster pulled a face at that. They reached a set of double doors, pressed a button on the wall and pushed open the doors. 'So here it is.'

Unbelievable. This wasn't a ward, it was . . . amazing! It was like something from a film, it was almost sci-fi. There was a brand new smell about the place, like something unwrapped for the first time.

Sister Brewster opened the door of one room and gestured Megan in.

'Flat-screen TV for everyone, so no fights over programmes.' She closed the door again. 'There's internet access, laptop computers, we've got musical instruments, PlayStations . . .'

Megan caught sight of movement on a nearby roof outside. 'There's a cat!'

Sister Brewster glanced at it before moving on. 'Oh, that old thing. Been around for ever. We call him Mr Henry.'

Megan followed, grinning, not able to take her eyes off it. 'Really?' She thought of Kipper and Jackson and her heart filled.

'We've got quite a few strays around the place. They're all called Mr Henry. It's easier. Now then, look at this.' A door was swept open to reveal a kitchen. 'For all those burgers and things you all seem to want. Pizzas. Over here,' Sister Brewster breezed past her, 'is the Graffiti Wall. We're getting an artist in once we open to do some work with patients.'

'Wow!' Everything was gleaming, sprayed with newness. In one corner was a huge purple beanbag. Megan went over to it, poked her finger into it. There was a rustle, a squeak. She plonked herself down and it moulded into her. She let out a delighted whoop. 'This is – fab, it's like a posh hotel!'

'Yes, isn't it?' Sister Brewster smiled. 'We're all very pleased about it. No doubt there'll be teething problems when we get going, but I'm sure we can iron those out.'

Megan heaved herself back out of the beanbag, rearranged it, punched out the cave her body had made, the echo of herself. There was a corner with a sofa and easy chairs, a coffee table and . . . 'Is that one of those jukebox things?'

'Exactly what it is. Bit sparkly, isn't it! Lots of music on it. Some I even recognise.' She gave a smile. 'I expect we'll be able to use these CDs in it. Not that I know how to work it. But someone will.'

Sister Brewster placed Megan's pile of CDs and DVDs on a shelf next to the jukebox. 'That's great.

Thanks for these. A good start for our collection. And here . . .' There was another room with soft chairs and a rug, and shelves ready to be filled. 'Quiet study . . . or just somewhere away from everyone else.' She clasped her hands together and gazed down at Megan, face serious. 'Well, do you like it? Do you think people your age would like it?'

Megan nodded, still amazed, still looking around. 'It's just great.'

'We think young people with cancer will do well in a place like this. They'll feel better about being in hospital. Do you think they will?'

It was hard to take it all in, hard to answer. 'But . . . what about all the treatment and stuff? They must have to go somewhere else to get that . . .'

Sister Brewster shook her head. 'All done here.' It seemed so simple, so wonderful.

Megan stood in the middle of the unit absorbing everything. A thought struck her. 'How did it all happen so quickly?'

'Well, units like this cost over a million pounds to build new, but they completely gutted the old Outpatients Department. The builders have been here for ever. I'm surprised you didn't notice . . . on your travels.'

Megan smiled. How did she miss this?

'Then we got some additional funding . . .' Sister Brewster spread her hands as if to take in the whole place. 'You'll see who from when we go out.

So, anyway, this is it. We get our first patients in next month. They'll be coming from all over the place. This is the quietest it's ever going to be, I imagine!' They were making their way back to the entrance now.

'Will you be working here?' Megan asked.

'Well, yes, actually.' Sister Brewster smiled. 'Can't think why. There were a couple of teenagers I had to look after once, I remember. Nothing but trouble.' Megan could feel herself blush. 'But they were two of the nicest people I've met and one in particular is still talked about by cleaners, consultants, the mortuary technician . . .'

So it hadn't been stories after all! Good old Jackson!

They were heading back towards the doors, towards the real world of hospitals, out from the magical place that was the new unit for teenagers. Sister Brewster pressed another button and they pushed back through the double doors. She paused by the plaque on the wall. It was made of polished wood with words cut into it, painted gold. Megan read the inscription, felt her eyes sting, felt her whole body almost crumble.

'Well, what do you think?'

Megan could say nothing at all, she was so full of pride and love and wishing.

Sister Brewster put an arm around her shoulder. 'I know,' she said. 'That's what I think too.'

Nineteen

Megan pushed open the garden gate. Dad must still be in bed. Or in the bath. He liked to have a long steep, just like Mum, with lots of bubbles. He said it was never the same when he was away. The baths were never as nice as home.

She didn't go into the house, but sat on the seat Dad had made under the big tree. Somehow she couldn't seem to think straight. Perhaps it was the visit to the hospital. Perhaps it was seeing the unit, seeing the staff again, but her head seemed full of pictures and sounds, memories and questions, all flying about like jigsaw pieces and she couldn't solve any of it.

She closed her eyes against the sun and she was there in the middle of it all, trying to sort it out. A squeal of rubber on the floor. She knew that sound. A wheelchair. Yes. She was lying on a bed with all sorts of machines around her, bleeping and wheezing. The room seemed full of people, their words scrambled. Yet beneath it all was someone talking in a low, mysterious voice.

There was a famine in the land, and for months, no rain. Day after day the sun burn in the cloudless skies, the grass parch like a coffee berry. The trees also parch, and brown, same way. . . .

There were murmurs, soft movements. Hushes and whispers. Footsteps. Sister Brewster's maybe, or Siobhan's. Or was it someone new? Where was this, exactly? She recognised Mum's shoes with the low heel which clipped along the floor, and Dad's lace-ups, creaking as he walked. There was a cough. Someone sniffing. The voice carried on in snatches. Some of it she caught, some of it drifted away.

. . . Mister Anancy get up, next morning, dress in a long coat, tall hat and black bag, and he set off to Fish Country. When he get there, he take him an office, hang up a signpost: M. Anancy. Surgeon *. . .*

Megan tried to find Jackson. It was his voice, but there was only darkness. Yet he was there, filling the place, talking like an old man from a faraway land.

. . . his first patient is very large fish . . . Anancy

look in her eye from all angle, he take a long, long,
time . . . suddenly he just come up and say, 'Your eye
they is weak, but I think I can help you . . .'

Megan moved in and out of the story as the words
fell around her. There was some trick the spider
played and money to be paid and oh she wanted to
hang on to all those words, because it was Jackson,
in the room, close by, close enough to touch.

. . . and the fool, fool, fish pay him and he set off
on his journey home . . . Anancy dash across the
river . . .

More movements. The air hissed with whispers.
Jackson's voice began to trail away as the story
reached its end. There was that squeal of rubber
again, the wheels of his chair swinging round, the
sound drifting away and away.

Another door. Her own back door. Dad was striding
towards her, in his sunglasses, his shirt sleeves
rolled up, showing his tanned arms. He looked big
and strong.

'Hello. You're in a world of your own.' He sat
down next to her on the seat. 'What's wrong? If it's
to do with Grandad, then, don't worry. We can sort
it out.'

Megan wiped her eyes. 'It's not. It's just . . . I
remembered the story Jackson told. Bits of it,
anyway.' She slipped her arm through Dad's. He
squeezed it. 'It was about a fish,' she went on.

'Anancy cheats a fish out of its money. He pretends he's a doctor. Was that it? Something like it?'

Dad frowned. 'You know, I think it was. I mean, he had this funny accent, which made it hard to grasp, but that was the gist of it, I think.'

Megan smiled. 'I knew it.'

'Well, I never,' Dad said. 'Fancy you remembering that.'

'And where was I? Not in my own room. Was I somewhere different?'

Dad paused, looking uncomfortable. He stared into the distance. 'We used to call it Intensive Care . . .' He looked at her, his eyes glistening, face drawn, as if in pain. 'Oh, you were so ill, love.'

Megan pressed into him, leaning her head on his shoulder. 'But I'm better now, Dad,' she said, 'you know I am.' She'd won her battle, that's what people said, yet it felt like a poor victory when Jackson didn't, when Kipper didn't.

Dad was blinking as if the sun were in his eyes. 'Yes, you are, thank God.'

They sat for a while in silence.

'So, where did you go off to, so early this morning? I woke up to find you gone. Didn't want to pry, with you being so upset last night, but now, you say you're better, so I'm asking.' He raised his eyebrows and peered over the top of his sunglasses at her.

'I went to the hospital. To the new unit.'

Dad looked surprised. 'Did you really? I thought you didn't want to.'

'I didn't. But there's this direct bus now, and I got on it.' It seemed unbelievable, even though it was only an hour or so since she was there. 'I just decided to go.'

There was a sigh. 'You were very brave to do it on your own.'

More silence, though all around them the garden was alive with birds.

Dad looked at his watch at last. 'One of us needs to be getting on with things. There's a party to go to.' He turned to Megan. 'You know, when this is all over and you're back at school and everything, there'll be shape to the days, a getting-up time, a going-to-bed time. You'll be able to get back to something like normal. Start living your life again. And I know everyone says it, but I think you can.' Dad said this as if he hoped it really could happen. 'I know you can.'

Megan wasn't so sure. 'At the new unit, they've got this plaque, with gold letters and everything. And Jackson's name. They've called it the Jackson Dawes Unit. Sister Brewster showed me.

'They got some money from Jackson's family. It was his. I mean, it would have been his, when he was twenty-one.'

Dad turned to look into her face, his eyes holding

217

hers steadily. 'Would he have liked it, do you think? Approved of it?'

'Yes,' Megan said, 'he'd have liked it, but I wish . . .'

'What do you wish, love?'

How to put it into words. Wishing for the impossible was such a waste of time and yet . . .

'I hope Jackson died happy,' she rushed on. 'He wanted to do so many things and be alive and everything, so I don't know how he could have been happy, but I hope he was all right about it. I hope so.'

This was it. The thing she didn't know and couldn't solve. Like a puzzle, with one piece missing. It had been there, worming around inside her, since who knew when, and only now was she able to catch it, pin it down.

If only she could know that he'd been all right about it.

Then her surviving wouldn't seem so bad.

And Grandad having a party on Sunday, with all the Poor Old Souls going to dance and sing and eat sausage rolls. And people saying he was amazing, ninety-six was so old.

Because it was Jackson and Kipper who were really the amazing ones, wasn't it? And all the others who *didn't* survive?

Dad pushed his hands into his pockets. 'Megan, did you read the letter Jackson's sister sent?' She nodded, feeling bleaker than winter. 'I don't mean just the bit that told you he'd died. Did you read it all? Have you read it through to the very end?'

'No.' Megan froze, as if he'd splashed her with something, as if he was just about to do it again. 'I don't want to . . . I don't *have* to.'

There was no point.

Nothing was going to change.

The letter had been her constant companion since it came, but she should have thrown the horrible thing away.

Dad stood there, solidly. 'Where is it, love?' Megan refused to answer, like a stubborn child. 'Is it in your bedroom? Did you throw it away?' He waited as if there wasn't a train to catch, a party to go to, as if he had all the time in the world.

At last, Megan pulled the tightly folded square from her pocket and thrust it at him. She didn't want it any more. What was the point of carrying it around with her like that? Like some stupid girl with a crush, like some rubbish problem-page person, like it was part of her.

It wasn't going to bring Jackson back.

'*I* know what it says. Mum read it out to me on the phone. *All* of it.' Dad looked around the garden as if in search of the answer to an impossible question. 'But *you* don't know and you've never let Mum talk about it and to be perfectly frank, I think you've been a bit silly. *More* than a bit silly.' The small blue vein at his temple looked rigid, his lips were pressed into a thin line.

How dare he be angry? When she was the one who'd had her head cut open, and had chemo and everything, and lost Jackson, and her place on the football team, and her hair, and poor Kipper, and oh, the list was so long she could wrap it round the world. How dare he be angry with her?

The letter stuck to her hand, she could feel it almost welding to her fingers.

Dad relaxed slightly. 'Look,' he said. 'I just want you to see the whole picture, that's all, not just the bits that hurt. It doesn't all hurt. You can't let it all hurt.'

Megan said nothing. It did hurt. All of it.

'I've got to go and get ready.' Dad sighed, as if it was all suddenly too much to cope with and he wished Mum was here to take over. 'There's a train to catch. I'd like it if you'd come to Grandad's, but . . .' he touched her cheek gently though his face was set like stone, 'that's not so important. You'll be OK with Gemma. I can speak to her mum. What's important is that you take some time, right now, and read that letter, right to the last word. Do you hear? I don't want you coming through that door till you have.'

Turning his back on her, he walked into the house.

Megan watched, mouth open.

Dad never ordered her around. He was the soft one, the cuddly one, who came home from work with presents and was jolly and fun and left things like bills and cooking and rules up to Mum. He never told her off. He never made her do stuff she didn't want to.

Yet here he was, ordering her to do something she couldn't.

Twenty

The garden was filled with ordinary, everyday noises. There were children playing somewhere along the street, and a dog skittered by chasing a ball. Nothing felt ordinary inside. She was apart from it all, an outsider looking in. Or perhaps the other way around.

Megan unfolded the letter, smoothing out the deep lines which were scored into the paper so that it looked like lots of small squares stuck together, not very securely.

Like me, she thought.

Glancing back at the house, she saw Dad in the kitchen. He was on the phone. Probably talking to Mum. His voice drifted through the window, chatting away as if nothing had happened. Or everything.

The letter flapped slightly in the breeze as if to remind her of its presence. There was no point in not reading it. It couldn't hurt any more than it did when it first came. Megan leaned up against the tree, its branches heavy with leaves, but already they were changing colour. One or two had fallen to the ground. Things were moving on. She spread open the letter, smoothed it straight.

Dear Mrs Bright,

My mother has asked me to write and tell you that Jackson lost his fight with cancer last week. She thought you might like to know and that you could tell Megan.

The hospital did all they could, but as my mother says, there was another plan for Jackson and we have to accept it. We are trying not to be sad. Jackson wouldn't want that, but we miss him very much, his good humour, his smile. You met him, so you know what I mean.

It's very hard for my mother, of course, but she wanted you to know that Jackson never stopped talking about Megan. We all think she made his illness and the end of his life so much easier for him. My mother says Megan was there with him, in his mind and in his heart, and she thanks God for the gladness she gave him, and for helping him through. She was there when he needed her, and that made him happy.

Please let her know how grateful we all are for that. We hope that Megan is well, and stays well.
On behalf of Elvira Dawes,
Josephine Dawes

The handwriting was perfect, as if Josephine Dawes had taken a lot of care, as if Mrs Dawes, round as a dumpling, had stood at her daughter's shoulder, telling her exactly what to put, which words to use, and how to say them. They were plain and to the point. Not hiding anything, not making it sound better than it was. It must have broken their hearts to have to do such a thing. It must have burned right into them, to have to send such a letter.

Megan gazed at the words now, to soak them up, to feel the work that had gone into them, the respect, and love. Because Jackson's family did love him. Somewhere along the way she'd forgotten that. And they'd lost him. No wonder Dad was angry with her, when they'd had to sit down and write those words and she'd refused to read them properly.

At last she folded it very carefully, back along the lines Mum had made.

It wasn't a horrible letter at all.

It was a lovely letter.

She didn't hate it, not one bit of it, not even the words which told her that Jackson was dead.

Putting it back into her pocket, Megan found something else. It was the picture she'd finished the night of his operation. Just larger than a thumbnail sketch. She'd cut it out and kept it close to her since the letter had arrived, a ritual of remembering, as regular as cleaning her teeth, or washing her face. Yet, she'd refused to look at it as much as she'd refused to read the letter.

With a shock, she realised just how crumpled it had become. If she continued carrying it around like that, it would be ruined. And this was all there was of Jackson.

She looked at him now, in the afternoon sun. She'd managed to capture some of the life in his eyes, the happiness beaming out from his face, as if it would never leave him.

'You were too young,' she whispered.

He looked as if he didn't mind being young, or being crumpled, or stuffed into her pocket. *It's cool*, he seemed to be saying.

Don't worry about me.

I'm doing OK.

I'm in a place where the bees don't sting,
and the sun don't burn,
and there's no more trouble and pain.

Megan gazed at the picture, absorbing the lines and curves of his face, so that her eyes and her head, her heart and her skin were full of him, never to be erased, capturing the echoes of him, the memories of him, so that he was still here with her.

There was movement in the kitchen. Megan

looked over to find Dad watching her from the window, wanting everything to be all right. He would be leaving in a few hours. and he wanted her on the train with him. He looked so alone standing there, so worried.

If she could tell him she was OK, show him, then it would make him feel better, and Mum and Grandad, all the people who'd been worrying about her. All they were trying to do was move on, as if they'd had cancer too. Yet they wouldn't, not without her. And that's how it would stay, that's how it would be, until she gave the word, the sign.

It was up to Megan.

The air was still. Not a leaf moved. There were no birds, no sounds. It was like being in a bubble again, and all around it the world was clamouring to get in. She had to let the world in. She had to give the sign, say the word, take control again.

It wouldn't be so hard to get the train with Dad, go to the party, celebrate.

It wouldn't be so hard to write to Jackson's family, thank them, for taking the time to send her the letter. Maybe she could give them his picture. A copy of it.

She could do all that.

The air around her moved, as if given permission to. A small breeze riffled the leaves, breathing them to life.

But there was just one thing.

None of this could happen until she spoke to

Gemma and told her everything. It would have to start with Gemma.

Megan took out her mobile. It was the first number that came up. Always had been. Always would be.

'Gemma?'

There was a pause, like that gap after a flash of lightning, before the thunder comes, a pause which leaves you hoping that the crash won't be too loud, too frightening. Megan wondered if Gemma would just switch off her phone, refuse to answer. She wouldn't blame her, wouldn't be surprised. What more did she deserve?

'Hi.' Gemma's voice was low, flat. 'You still haven't gone, then?'

It felt like an accusation.

'I'm on the six o'clock train.' It was the truth. No more lies. 'I've got to get packed and everything, but . . .'

A car engine screeched just then and a crowd of birds exploded from next door's tree. Megan had never seen so many in one go. She watched them melt into the sky as if they'd never existed.

'Are you still there? Megan?'

'Sorry. Yeah. I was going to ask . . . if I can come over. For a little while? Once I've packed my stuff.'

'. . . OK . . .' Gemma didn't sound very sure, as if this might be a nasty trick and *she* wasn't to be trusted any more. Her best friend and everything.

'It's just . . . I need to tell you something.'

And then she began to cry, because it came to her, as suddenly as those birds from out of the tree, that Gemma would have understood, if only she'd told her before.

Weeks ago.

Months ago.

She would have known what to say.

It wasn't about cancer or having a tumour or chemo. Things her friends were scared of. This was just about a boy. And they could have laughed together about Jackson, about all the things he said and did, about all that trouble he got himself into.

And then they could have cried together.

It would have felt better.

But here she was on her own. Crying.

'Megan? What's wrong? I'm coming round. Right now.' Gemma. All hurt forgotten. Gemma, who couldn't bear to know anyone was upset, least of all her best friend.

'No, it's OK . . . I need to . . . tell you about someone I met,' Megan said, at last, dragging a hand across her eyes. 'Someone in hospital.'

Another pause. As if Gemma herself had tried to solve an unsolvable puzzle, just as she had done, and now the missing piece was found.

'What's his name?' Gemma asked, her voice gentle. Of course, she would know it was a boy, without being told.

The world seemed to shift then, as if for so long it

229

had been blown out of place by some awful earthquake or a volcano. It was settling back to where it should be. It would never be quite the same. How could it? But somehow, that was enough.

'Jackson,' Megan began, as if there was a long, long story to tell. 'He was called Jackson Dawes.'

Jackson Dawes, he's as tall as doors,
standing in his battered old hat,
singing his battered old songs,
slapping his fingers down the length of the stand
like an upright bass.
Badum, dum, dum, dum; badum, dum, dum, dum.
His hips swing gently,
his head nods,
his smile is wide,
big as the sun,
as if this is just any other day,
as if the world can't get any better,
as if the future is brighter than stars.

My Inspiration for
Anthem for Jackson Dawes

What inspired me to write this book? That's such a hard question to answer. As for pinpointing the exact date or time when the inspiration came, I can't do it. I don't know if I was sitting on a bus or a train, or just staring out of a window at home. I don't know if I saw a picture, or watched a film or read a book, or just gazed out into space instead of working. I certainly wasn't sitting in a children's cancer ward and I'm fairly sure that a sudden light did not flick on in my head. My brain doesn't work like that.

The story emerged, is all I can say, from a whole series of stories swimming around inside me. It floated to the top sometimes, then drifted away again like some kind of mysterious fish. Perhaps it would never have been caught and the story never written if it wasn't for some very good people who said, *That's the story you want. That one there, about a girl and a boy who meet in hospital.*

Thank goodness for those people, because they were right. I know about hospitals, having worked in them. I know about young people because once I was one and still remember how hard it can be sometimes. I know about illness and how it can affect a person. And writing about the things you know is usually the best place to start.

But I didn't want the story to be confined to two young people being stuck on a children's ward. I couldn't just write about Megan and Jackson, when they had mums and dads and friends who were all affected by their being in hospital. I couldn't just write about how Megan and Jackson felt, which was pretty bad at times, without thinking through and exploring how their families and friends felt, which was also pretty bad.

We all feel stranded sometimes, like travellers washed up on an island with no hope of getting off. Sometimes we forget that there are people who love us and care about us and will try all they can to help. Sometimes we forget that we are stronger than we know. I think Megan and Jackson were much stronger than they knew.

Perhaps they inspired me.

Yes. I think that may be the answer.

Celia Bryce

Acknowledgements

With grateful thanks to: Sam Smith, Teenage Cancer Trust Nurse Consultant (The Christie NHS Foundation Trust, Manchester), who read various extracts of the book, and advised on medical and nursing procedures. Sandra Barlow, Senior Sister (Teenage Cancer Unit, Royal Victoria Infirmary, Newcastle), who showed me around the amazing unit on Tyneside. Doctor Kate Hodges, Doctor Steve Hodges and Nurse Paul Heslop, who helped me with various other hospital details. My very good writing friends, Sonia Royal, Dorothy Brownlee and Michael Doolan, who read my manuscript and gave their valuable opinions and critical analysis. Young friends and relations, Sara Bradshaw, Amy Brown, Kate Hudson, Lucy Hudson and Kate Walmsley, who took the time, over the years it has taken to write this book, to read one or more of its many drafts and to give me their thoughts on the story. Members of the Marsden Writers' Group, who have patiently followed every step of this amazing writing journey. Helen Corner and Kathryn Price, at Cornerstones Literary Consultancy, who gave me superb editorial advice when the story was still very new and needed lots of rewriting. James Catchpole, at the Celia Catchpole Literary Agency, who had enough faith in Megan and Jackson's story to take me on and who then worked tirelessly at finding me a publisher. Emma Matthewson and the editing staff at Bloomsbury, who have worked with me over the last eighteen months, fine-tuning and polishing my manuscript, turning it into a book I can be proud of and making me a very happy writer indeed. My husband, Colin, and daughters, Lucy and Kate, who have given me their unwavering support and who, I know, will always share my writing dream. And finally, very special and heartfelt thanks to the families of Deanna and Vaila, who kindly allowed me to dedicate this book to them.